A Santa Stabbing

Dedication

To Steve, Alex and Ellen, as always

Chapter One

"**H**ELLO!" A SHRIEK that sounds like an opera singer doing a full-on soprano scale breaks through my early Saturday-morning shower reverie. My scrubbing hands still on my soapy scalp. I know it's Ralph who cried out. Ralph is my ten-year-old Amazon parrot—think the green bird on a pirate's shoulder—with exceptional vocal skills. He's also a spectacular watch bird. He's in his cage in the family room, which means there's a stranger nearby. Maybe knocking on the door of our second-and-third-floor home, above my shop. But most likely on the street one floor below. Nothing to get worked up over.

I go back to shampooing my hair, reveling in the Christmas shampoo's peppermint scent. It's still two weeks before Thanksgiving, but I'm all about the season this year—spiritually and commercially.

"I said 'helloooo!'" Ralph's tone is more strident, his volume full blast. I swear I feel my adrenals squeeze out heart-pumping hormones. There's somebody either outside the front door, or—*gulp*—in my apartment.

What if it's a robber? Or worse?

It's not a robber. This is Stonebridge, Pennsylvania, not Highway 101 in Northern California. Where seemingly sleepy bedroom communities—

No. I stop my overactive brain before it trips into a neighborhood I should never go. The one that shows up after I binge three Netflix true-crime documentaries. As I did last night. And maybe the night before.

Okay, I admit it. Since I dropped the girls off at college a few months ago, I've been spending the nights with some of the most notorious serial killers of all time. And I believe I have the real Jack the Ripper identified, someone never discovered—

"Owwww!"

Another ear-shredding shriek from Ralph, imitating my cry when he occasionally nips me. It's Ralph's code for *I mean it, Mom!*

Is someone in the apartment?

I shut off the water and stand stock still, assessing my options. A first glance around the newly renovated bathroom yields a sucky arsenal. The best weapon I have that would knock someone out cold is a solid linden wood carved Santa figure, but it's perched on a curio table next to the front door. A serial killer—*no, not a serial killer*—is between Santa dude and me. I've got to find something in the bath—

"Bad bird!" Ralph's voice, able to mimic any human voice with eerie accuracy, sounds exactly like my very angry, very serious self. His cry is followed by a distinct *thump.*

As in a heavy footfall.

My heartbeat trips into clanging. Someone's definitely in my apartment. I'm hot and cold all at once.

My second, frenzied gaze lands on the gargantuan bottle of salon-quality shampoo from Costco, shoved into the corner for the season as Candy Cane Locks takes center stage. The huge economy-sized bottle seemed like a treasure find after years of limited shampoo choices while I was stationed overseas. My bow to consumerism may be all that saves me. Will a plastic bottle weighing five pounds do it?

Of course it will. I've been to war and back. I've flown Navy helicopters through treacherous missions. I can make a large bottle of discount shampoo from Costco work. I bend over and reach for the bottle with soapy hands, clutch it to my—

"Don't worry, Angel, it's just me!" Mom's shout reaches me inside the shower and triggers the scream I'd shoved down moments earlier. The shampoo bottle slips from my hold and slams against my big toe. I yelp, the pitch higher than my first scream.

"Angel, what on earth?" Mom's in my bathroom, on the other side of the glass shower door, still holding her purse.

"*Mom!* Turn around. Please."

To her credit, Mom's quick on her feet and complies, but now she's facing the wide mirror which, yeah, reflects me behind the glass door. In all my sudsy glory.

"I'm sorry, Angel, I rang the bell and knocked several

times. And I thought you'd hear Ralph."

"I did hear Ralph." Talking through clenched teeth has become more regular since I moved back to my hometown. Especially with Mom. The well-meaning not-an-intruder. Kind of.

"Why don't I make a pot of coffee while you finish up? Take your time." Mom no doubt feels waves of my ire through the tempered glass. She leaves, and I lean against the shower wall to catch my breath.

But the tile is cold, soap is dripping in my eyes, and I'm shivering. I turn the water back on and let the heat wash away my annoyance.

I love my Mom. I love my Mom. I love my Mom.

FIVE MINUTES LATER, I walk into the kitchen, dressed in jeans and a sweater with JINGLE JINGLE in glitter cursive written across the chest. Mom's at the table, looking at her phone and sipping from my RUNWAYS ARE FOR BEAUTY QUEENS mug, a memento of my helicopter days when the only runway that mattered to me was onboard an aircraft carrier. I grab a white porcelain mug imprinted with holly leaves that I bought at the Luxembourg Villeroy & Boch outlet for one euro. It might only be mid-November, but with my shop opening soon, I'd committed to Christmas, 24/7 in September. I figured if I'm going to launch a new business, a new life, at the height of the season, I needed the long warm-up.

Mom's face lights up the minute she sees me, as if I'm the sole source of her happiness. Since I'm the youngest of three and she adores my brother and sister, I know it's not true, but for now I'll take it. Ignoring any lingering annoyance from her break-in, I drop a kiss on the top of her head. She's dressed in a cute white-and-blue-striped button-down, worn over her jeans with the sparkly threads.

"You look great, Mom."

"Thank you. You know I try. You slept in a bit today, didn't you? Good for you. Rest won't be easy to catch once the store opens." People have asked me over the years how I survived the rigors of the Naval Academy. They wouldn't ask if they'd met my mother. She's a bundle of energy from the moment her feet hit the floor before dawn.

Mom's bright amber eyes match mine, and I suspect that if I ever decide to stop dying my hair—chestnut number ten—I'll have her striking silver streaks, which she shows off in a shoulder-length bob.

"I'm fine, Mom." I purposefully overlook the jab about sleeping in. It's not yet eight on a Saturday, and my shop isn't open for business yet.

"Sit down with me." She motions to the kitchen table.

So much for my plans to sit upstairs on the balcony with Ralph and my first cup of the day. I remind myself that it's a blessing to be back in my hometown after twenty-plus years of globetrotting. Most importantly, it's great to be near my family again. Isn't this what I want to have with Ava and Lily years from now?

I won't be a stalker mother, will I?

Sipping as I sit down, a sweet, spicy flavor hits my tongue.

"You put cinnamon in it." Warmth rushes into my chest, and just like that, I'm grateful Mom busted in on my Saturday morning. I take a deep gulp. "Mmm."

"Your father won't drink it without a solid tablespoon over the grounds." She started adding the secret ingredient years ago when someone told her it'd keep an hours-old pot of coffee from turning bitter.

"Is Dad golfing?" A rhetorical question. Dad's always on the course on Saturdays. And any other day that isn't snow-covered or rained out. Which in south central Pennsylvania equates to approximately two-hundred-plus days per year.

"Yes, but he's going to wrap up at noon. We've got a date." Mom smiles as if she's sixteen instead of sixty-seven. "We're driving down to Baltimore later for dinner."

"Nice! But a long drive home after."

"Oh, no. We're staying at the Sagamore Pendry." Mom glances away as blush crosses her cheeks, still smooth thanks to copious amounts of sunscreen, moisturizer, and Grandma's genes.

"Oh." We're too close to TMI. I'm happy for my parents, grateful they are still enjoying…you know. But spare me the deets. "I'm glad you're taking time for yourselves."

"Me, too." Joy emanates from my mom like the sunshine gleaming off the granite countertops. "Have you got all you need set for the shop's first day? I was hoping we could go over your plans for the grand opening party."

I smooth my hands over the table's solid wood surface. "My goal is Small Business Saturday, I was hoping for a soft opening a few days sooner but decided to focus on one big day." The Saturday after Thanksgiving is only two weeks away, but I remind myself it's a target, not set in stone. I can open earlier, or later, if need be. One thing I want to do differently from my previous career is not put so much pressure on myself, not get backed into deadline corners. In the Navy, deadlines often mean life or death. In the civilian retail world, they mean being able to pay my employees and put food on my table. Important, absolutely. But not the same as having enemies put their crosshairs on you.

"Okay, then. It's your store, of course." It has to be killing Mom to not express her thoughts, not chastise me for ignoring any kind of formal schedule. She's all about planning. "You know I'm here, ready to help. At least let me order the cake."

"Actually, I was going to get an assortment of treats from different places. Baklava from Hellenic Café, Tiramisu cups from Ducci's Dolcis, chocolates from Belgian Bites. And for the more traditional, I'll get pies and such from Applebaum's Farmers Market." Supporting local business is the name of the game in Stonebridge. In turn, I hope they'll send my shop some love in the form of customers. "I'm thinking of running out there this morning." I wasn't, really, but I knew it would calm Mom down if she thought I was on top of it.

"Great idea, Angel. I'll put on my thinking cap to come up with a few more."

"Thanks, Mom."

Mom grins, and we sit in comfortable silence for a few heartbeats.

"I know you don't like me to bring it up, but how are you really doing, honey, with the girls gone? You haven't been alone since Tom passed. Not really." Sure enough, Mom can't keep her internal dialogue internal.

"I'm good, Mom." No, I don't want to talk about it. Do I miss Tom? Yes. Am I over the grief of losing him five years ago to a rare form of incurable cancer? Can one ever be? But I'm not *not* over it, either. Shop 'Round the World will allow me to keep him close, as we did so much curio collecting together. Our sentimental treasures are the inspiration for my stock.

"You need to talk about it, Angel." Mom's mistaken my quiet for angst.

"I appreciate your concern and support, Mom. I know you're here, and it means a lot. If I need to talk, I will." I focus on my coffee, which needs another pour of half-and-half.

Mom finally hears me and backs off, whistling at Ralph,

who ignores her. His insouciant parrot attitude reflects in his deliberate silence, how he glares at Mom. Rude, but I get it. *If she's not breaking into the house, why bother?*

"Have you met up with any of your local friends yet?" Mom can't let go.

"There hasn't been time." When Mom says "friends" all I see in my mind's eye are the several high school classmates who also own small businesses in town. All great folks, don't get me wrong, but at this point another box to fill on my long to-do spreadsheet. They've been pressuring me to attend the local small business association, the Stonebridge Business Buddies, meetings. "I'll have plenty of time to get with my friends once I get the store going."

"Hmm." Mom finishes her coffee and takes her mug to the sink. "I've learned that we have to make the time for fun, or it won't happen. I understand that you're under the gun while you set up shop, but you're not in the Navy anymore, Angel. You're in business for yourself. It's okay to take some time off. You keep saying you're going to get back to flying. And don't overlook the networking opportunities friends bring."

"I won't. Thanks, Mom." I don't bother to remind her that while I have a private pilot's license, I do not have my own plane and flight hours aren't cheap.

We hug and she scoots off, on her way to Skeins and Baahls, the local yarn shop owned by my older brother Bryce and his husband Nico. I haven't been in their quaint shop nearly enough these past weeks. I enjoy knitting, but I'm channeling all of my creative energies into the store. It's going to have to be enough fun for now.

I finish getting ready in the quiet, and find it unhinges me. No matter how much I remind myself that I'm safe, that it was Mom who "broke in," my sympathetic nervous system is still in overdrive. Not unlike the aftermath from a dangerous flight mission.

Yeah, I need to trade my Netflix serial killer binges for the home decorating channel.

Chapter Two

MY SISTER PHONES as Ralph and I enter the shop twenty minutes later. I press my wireless headset's button.

"Hey, Crystal."

"Good morning, Sunshine!" My older sister's exuberant energy is the perfect antidote to my often too-serious countenance. "How's it going?"

"Good. Mom just left."

"You're kidding. How early did she get there? Did she wake you up?"

"She scared me at first, because I was in the shower. I wish she'd get the *text-first* thing down."

"Tell me about it. She almost caught Brad and I...you know." She snorts. "No offense, but I'm relieved she's got an extra life to direct. Takes a bit of the pressure off me and Bryce, you know?"

"Trust me, she was equally adept at long-distance manipulation." We laugh. I have zero business whining over Mom's irreverence toward personal boundaries. Crystal's right. It's about time I came back and took some of the pressure off of her and our brother Bryce. Mom's motive is always love, but she can come across like a sledgehammer.

"Did she mention where she's headed next?"

"To the yarn shop. The Saturday Stitchy Sisters." It's the knitting group that meets at Bryce's yarn shop.

"Did you tell her about our coffee date?"

"Nope. She'll be stitching while we catch up." We chuckle in sisterly commiseration. Doing things with Mom is great, but we need our private girl talk, too.

"I'm already in the shop." I try without success to keep the impatience out of my tone. It's almost nine o'clock; I'm used to starting my workday three hours earlier. Some military habits die harder than others, even on a Saturday.

"Did the contractor finish the shelving yesterday?"

I sigh. "No, and I'm not thrilled with what they've done so far. I asked for simple floating shelves all along the walls, yet the contractor kept trying to install bookshelf-type built-ins. They don't usually work on Saturdays, but Phil's agreed to fix it and finish in time for my grand opening, as per our contract. But...wait for it...they're not coming today; some emergency came up. Which means they'll still be here all next week." After doing such a spectacular job on my kitchen and bathroom, Phil had to peel off from the project to handle a larger home renovation and left me with what I'm coming to appreciate as his *B team*. Good, capable, but without the focus of their boss.

"Hold firm, Sis. Your vision is superb. I have faith in

you!" Crystal's serious, I kid you not. Big sis by birth order, spiritual shaman by choice, she's my self-appointed life coach. At least she thinks she is. I can lose patience with her encouragement, and I have to remind myself she's missed having me nearby for over twenty-two years. Save for our summer trips home and my family's infrequent visits to us, it's been a long haul. I've missed my family, too, but I did have my girls and the flying to keep me fully occupied. Not to mention the plethora of exotic duty destinations. And for precious parts of it, I had Tom.

Tom. My heart does that little squeeze I don't think it'll ever stop doing when I remember him.

"Thanks, Sis. See you later?"

"Yes. I'll be done with my morning deliveries by ten-thirty, see you then!" We'd agreed to meet when Crystal was done since it's her half-day, and I hoped to be well into stocking my new inventory. I'm looking forward to meeting her at Latte Love, Stonebridge's single fancy coffee shop. It's a new addition since two summers ago, and I have to say I've enjoyed the change from the bracing Navy coffee, a.k.a. battery acid, I was used to.

The call disconnects and I can get down to business.

"Let's do it, Ralph."

Ralph mimics my laughter perfectly, followed by a quick "See you then!"

"You're a nosy old man, do you know that?" No one eavesdrops like my feathered buddy.

RALPH AND I walk through the front retail area to the back hallway that connects my office and a nice-sized storage area. The room is stuffed with boxes and cartons, all screaming for me to open them. Seeing stacks of boxes used to dismay me. After thirteen moves in twenty-two years, and the arduous work of unpacking every single item we owned each time, who can blame me for popping a hive or two at the sight of all that corrugated cardboard? But there's no corresponding squeal of packaging tape being ripped from its reel, no heavy scent of sweaty movers loading a truck parked awkwardly in front of our home. These boxes represent treasures I've spent a career finding.

"Hello." Ralph reminds me I'm holding him.

"Hey, sweetie pie. The workers aren't going to bother us today. Let's put your cage in the front room so that you can look out the window."

I place Ralph atop his open cage, then wheel it down the hall and into the center of the store. The entire front window is his view, which should keep him entertained. He fluffs his iridescent green feathers in approval.

Back in my office, I pull up the project manager software on my tablet, and do my best to ignore the fingers of loneliness that tug on my hard-won serenity.

I have my Navy tour in Belgium to thank for Shop 'Round the World. I had already acquired quite the holiday collection of ornaments from each duty station—Hawaii, Japan, Italy, San Diego, the UK, Washington State. But the Belgium tour catapulted my predilection to collecting pretty things into near hoarder status. If the Navy didn't put a weight limit on household goods, it would have been impossible for me to stop myself from adding more to my trove than I already had. But the collecting gave me the vision of a local shop filled to the brim with handcrafted treasures.

With the grand opening two weeks away, I have to focus on getting the stock inventoried and on display.

The back office is normally quite large—a mirror of the storage room. But the contractors have set up their wood shop in here, complete with a couple of scary looking saws atop both ends of a huge piece of plywood. Rustic sawhorses support it all.

I squeeze between the makeshift workbench and World War II–era industrial desk left by the previous owners to get to the stack of invoices I've printed.

There's no time to waste, as this is my first day in six without the incessant bang of hammers and whine of the super-sharp blades. I take a deep inhale and relish the scent of fresh cedar as I match invoice numbers with boxes. My gaze catches on an open box of recyclables and trash that I left in the middle of the floor last night, when I worked until almost midnight.

I function better in a clear space, so I open the back door

that leads to the low concrete stoop and place the box there, letting a decent breeze into the building for a few moments to clear the air. The loud *screech* of the hinges reminds me to get a can of lubricant to spray them. I don't go out this back door much, save for dumping trash.

As I lean over to set the box down, footsteps on the lightly graveled lot startle me. I straighten. A tall figure looms over me, blocking out the sun. This time it's not my mom.

"Hey!" My voice is loud and low, automatically back in Navy Commander mode. I take a step back, ready to slam the shop door closed. Yes, it's Stonebridge, PA, not Serial Killer, PA, but the back alley appears deserted.

The muscular dude spots me and halts. His eyes grow wide before he grins at me from under his Hershey Bears ski cap. It's Max, one of Phil's workers. Relief flows like Christmas morning through my veins, loosening my shoulders. Irritation blooms in my gut. Mom's unexpected appearance earlier still has me on edge.

"Whoa! Sorry, didn't mean to scare you. Wow. Glad I didn't whack you with one of these." His laugh sounds forced. I scared him as much as he did me. "Uh, the boss wanted me to swing by and drop these off for work first thing Monday." He lets out a breath, offers me another smile as he nods at the long planks in his arms. "We aim to get the shelves exactly how you want them, Ms. Warren."

My mouth opens to ask him to please call me Angel, then shuts. Annoyance tugs on my composure. I'd been hoping for uninterrupted work time this morning.

"I've no doubt you will, Max. I'd expect nothing less from Phil's team."

I swear his chest expands on command. Guess I still have the magic touch when it comes to empowering someone, even when I mistake them for a murderer.

"Uh, do you mind if I set these inside the shop?" Max still holds the heavy boards, and I move aside, opening the door wide for him. I figure he's about twenty-five, one of the oldest on Phil's B team.

"Go on in. Watch out for trip hazards."

"No problem."

He takes the boards to the front of the store. When he passes me his soap, cologne, or some other variety of body scent adjuster wafts around him. His collared shirt and dark, un-marked jeans indicate he's on his way to something other than work.

Max sets the boards down and straightens, his gaze resting on Ralph. I've kept Ralph upstairs when the carpenters are working. Paint fumes and wood shavings are toxic to avian lungs.

"Cool bird." He holds up his pointer finger to Ralph, perched atop his cage. Ralph shrinks away from the looming stranger.

"Careful! He bites."

"Really?" He frowns.

Max's disbelief doesn't surprise me. A lot of folks haven't

listened over the years, and got a nice quick nip from Ralph as a reward. Just enough pressure to let them know he could have broken skin if he wanted to. Maybe a bone, if it was a pinkie.

"Yes, myself included. With me they're mostly love bites because he's bonded with me. Ralph's not so friendly with everyone else."

"Okay, well, then…" He trails off, shoves his hands into his pockets. It strikes me that he seems a little lost, but I have to remind myself that he's not one of my sailors. Max doesn't work for me—he's employed by Phil. Thus, it's not my job to figure out what makes him tick.

"Thanks for dropping off the lumber, Max. See you Monday?" It's all I can do to not shove him out the door. I have to get back to the invoices.

"Sure thing, Ms. Warren." He lets himself out the back. I shove the box full of trash out the door and pull it tightly closed.

I spend the next hour unwrapping the dozens of wooden Santas that have arrived from one of my Russian handcrafts suppliers, matching them to the invoices. So far my Santa source, Tatyana, has sent me nothing less than exceptional product.

Which is why I'm less than thrilled with the Santas I'm unwrapping. They were supposed to be classic Russian Santas, hand carved and painted hardwood. I ordered only Christmas-themed *Dzed Moroze*, Father Snow, the Russian version of Santa Claus. Sweeping robe-like coats and matching hats, intricately carved staffs coated in gold paint held by mittened hands. Santa faces with rosy cheeks and bright eyes, boasting winding white-and-gray beards.

These are nowhere near what I ordered. This box of six-inch statues is full of Santas sporting various NFL logos, and their hats seem pointier than normal. Did she order from a new artist? Or mix my invoice up with another?

If these were nesting dolls instead of the Santa figures, I'd go with the flow. It's common to have various themed Matryoshka dolls; I've ordered several Pittsburgh, Philadelphia, and Pennsylvania pro- and college-team themes for the nesting collectibles. But my Santa inventory is meant to be top of the line, pure Christmas. I sigh, wondering if Tatyana has enough time to accept a return and get what I ordered delivered. I look at the whiteboard calendar on the office's far wall. It's possible, but the shipping might be cost prohibitive. I reach for my phone to call her—

"Ouch!" Ralph's shriek startles me. He must see someone in the front window. I don't hear knocks at the shop entry when I'm this far in the back. I spin on my foot to see who it is. My sudden movement catches my hip on the corner of the workbench, and the row of unwrapped Santas jiggles. Time slows as thousands of dollars of inventory threaten to jump off the plywood.

"No!" I reach over with both arms, stopping all but one of the football Santas from launching into midair. I watch in dismay as a Santa flips, hits the side of the contractor's buzz saw, and splits into two jagged pieces that hit the floor with two sickening thuds. I kneel and pick up the pieces of the destroyed Santa. And mentally calculate the cash loss.

Business isn't open yet, and I'm already destroying my profits. I throw the Santa halves into the box that rests against the back door. The tinkling crunch of the half-dozen malformed glass swizzle sticks I threw out last night underscores the weight of the broken Santa, and a shot of sadness slices through my hurried activity. An artisan in Russia spent hours perfecting the now unsaleable Santa. And there's nothing I can do about it.

It's part of being in retail.

I'm still on my knees, grasping the workbench to stand back up, when an unfamiliar clicking sound sounds, followed by a distinct scratching at the back employee-only door. Keys against the steel door. I stop breathing as my heart races. Mom has keys to the front door, to my apartment upstairs. No one else has the keys to this back entrance, except the girls and their keys are with them at their respective universities.

Someone's letting themselves in, picking the lock. All that separates us is a standard push-lever commercial door. I can always get out, but no one should be able to get in without a key.

Ralph's whistle echoes through the building.

It's his way of warning me.

I'm not going to let anyone think they can even try to get into my shop. Navy training kicks in as I cut to the chase and press the lever. The door flings open.

Chapter Three

"WHOA!" A WOMAN jumps backward, arms flailing, her feet miraculously staying under her. A paper cup flies through the air and *splats* onto the gravel. Steaming coffee splashes across the concrete stoop, rolling to a stop with the LATTE LOVE logo face up.

"What the he—!" Harshly spoken words have my hackles up, but I'm too stunned to reply. I've heard a lot of creative swearing onboard ships, but I have to admit, this particular string of epithets ranks among the saltiest. The woman's arms flail as she fights to stay upright. I reflexively grab at her, managing to catch her upper arm in one hand and coat lapel in the other.

"Let go of me!" She's not even fully upright before she yells at me, clearly surprised. Shocked, maybe.

I immediately recognize Frances Schrock, my high school classmate and owner of the real estate business that has basically bought and sold most of Stonebridge. Including my shop and home, the cutest red brick building on Main Street. Yes, I'm partial.

"Frannie! I'm so sorry. I, I thought you were a burglar." I

stare at the humongous collection of keys still grasped in her hand. Is the one clutched between her thumb and index finger a match to mine?

"Angel!" Her usual dulcet tone returns. "Oh my gosh, I didn't know you'd be here this morning or of course I would have knocked!" She shoves the keys into the pocket of her perfectly tailored wool coat and looks down to where her leather tote lay, piles of papers spilling out. "I was going to leave my brochures for the Stonebridge Tourism Authority on your desk."

At my silence, she shifts her feet. I'm being quiet because I'm trying to figure out how on earth, in any world, this is okay. That someone not connected to my business would think it's okay to break in—okay, let herself in—to leave brochures. I'm new to the small-town rules thing, after being gone for so long and living on a global scale. I'm not that out of touch, am I?

"Gosh, Angel, I'm so sorry I startled you. The whole point of me leaving these was to not bother you. I'm taking them to all the businesses in town today."

"Your coffee is gone."

"No worries whatsoever." She looks down at her outfit. "Look, not a drop on me. We're good."

There's a coffee stain on my brown leather boots, but I figure she doesn't notice it because she's busy shoving the papers into her bag. She straightens, her usually smooth face crinkled in…worry?

"Come on in while I get you a fresh cup. It's the least I can do." I hold the door open, wave her into my cramped office. "I've got my hot beverage bar all set up. Your choice, coffee or tea."

Frannie waves her hand in the air as if flitting away a gnat. "Please, are you kidding? That's not necessary. It's no biggie, seriously." But she follows my outstretched arm and enters my office. I shut the door firmly behind us, not desiring any more surprises this morning.

"I imagine you're wondering why I'd come here and let myself in, but believe me, it was because I didn't want to take up any of your time. I ran into your mother at Latte Love, and she mentioned you might be out this morning. When no one answered at the front door, I thought I'd try the back."

"It's okay." It isn't, but again, it's on me that I haven't changed the locks yet. "Coffee?"

Frannie nods. We stand at the beverage counter as I prepare her drink. I feel her gaze on me, and when I look up she draws in a breath, nods. "So tell me, Angel, how are you doing? I haven't seen you since the closing, except for out here on the street a time or two."

I wince inwardly, hoping she's not still upset that I worked with Dave, one of her more junior agents, instead of with her or her husband and business partner Ken. I'd been so anxious to seal the deal on my home and shop building that I'd not thought about contacting her directly. And in my defense, the junior agent had been the listing agent.

Frannie has assured me more than once that my oversight, like the coffee spill, wasn't *any big deal*, but my guilt lingers. It's too dang easy to make missteps returning to the community where I learned to ride a bike, had my first kiss, learned how to go after my heart's desires. I've been gone a long time.

"I'm good. Setting up my business, keeping myself beyond busy. I'm shooting for the grand opening in two weeks."

"I'm so glad to hear that. We're all thrilled that you picked Stonebridge as your permanent port-of-call. It's an honor to have a real-life Navy hero in our midst!"

True to Frannie's words, there's no sign of rancor in the wide smile she gives me. In fact, she's downright welcoming, as always.

"I'm no hero. Just did my job is all." I assume she's referring to the press release describing one of my combat missions. I flew a SAR mission that got six SEALs out of a sticky spot. It was a right-time, right-place thing as far as I'm concerned. I didn't fly into the thick of a battle, but the newspaper made it sound like I did.

"You're modest, just like Will." She refers to her son in the US Marine Corps. Her gaze is constantly looking past me, skittering about the office, as though she's hoping for someone more interesting to show up. I notice that her lipstick, a deep cinnamon, matches the autumnal hues of her outfit. She's making the most of the Thanksgiving season, while I'm already into Christmas. Frannie's always been the most stylish of all my high school classmates, garnering her the best-dressed award at the end of senior year. Her pumpkin gingham blouse's collar peeks out from under a matching orange crewneck sweater, all under a stylish ginger car coat that tops nutmeg corduroys. Her pants are tucked into mocha leather high-heeled boots. My comfy holiday sweater and battered jeans shoved into well-worn boots is shabby by comparison.

No negative self-talk allowed. You're still in setup mode. Besides, comparers never prosper, or something like that.

Frannie takes the holly-themed mug into her perfectly manicured hands and sits on the one additional chair in my office, intimating we'll have a prolonged chat. She chose pumpkin creamer for her coffee, and the scent of cinnamon fills the air.

"How are you doing, Frannie? How's Ken?"

"Me? I'm fine! Business is crazy, of course, as you know. Be glad you bought when you did. I just sold the building three down from yours for almost twice as much." Her enthusiasm is evident in the way her eyes sparkle and her teeth flash with each smile. Frannie leans on one hip, her bright blue eyes assessing me over her chic sunglasses.

"Your mother says you've got so many dreams for this old laundromat. I would have thought you'd still be working on your apartment. There's a reason you got the building for a song!" She emphasizes *dreams* as if they're mere wisps of ideas and not about to become my, and Stonebridge's only, international curio shop on Main Street. I trust my mother, as in I know she didn't say anything intimate to Frannie. But Frannie's job is to overstate the obvious, so it's easy for her to take a simple statement and blow it out of proportion. I'm unnerved by the reminder that nothing I do here is under the radar. Sure, I lived in a fishbowl while in military communities, but most of them were much larger than Stonebridge.

"My family helped me with the renovations, so the up-stairs living quarters are close to finished. And yes, I do have a lot of plans for the shop." I see her take in the disarray that is the temporary woodshop, her brow curved in disbelief. "This is all temporary, from the contractors. Some of my plans will take longer to implement than others. I'm sure you can relate, since you and Ken started up your real estate business from nothing."

"We did, but that was over twenty years ago, right out of college, when William was in pre-school. It seems a lifetime ago." She smiles and her lips tremble. She presses them together as if trying to rein in her momma-bear heart. "Now my boy's a Marine. I can't tell you how proud I am of him. And before I forget, thank you for your service. I never knew what a sacrifice it must have been for your parents to let you go when you were so young."

While I'm sure they had their concerns, my parents were

more than a teensy bit thrilled to have their bouncing-off-the-walls child out the door to chase her dream of becoming a Navy pilot. I'm not going to even try to explain this to Frannie, though. Not in a quick gab session, anyway. I don't know Frannie's son; I've only seen him in quick catch-ups like this one. He's almost five years older than the twins, as Frannie and Ken had him while they were still in college.

"William went straight into the Corps right out of high school, right? That's impressive. He's a brave young man. I had four years in Annapolis before I was one hundred percent in the Fleet."

"You're being too modest, Angel. You've always been that way. But now you're part of the Stonebridge small business scene." She leans forward, places a hand on my desk. "Can I share something? One thing you need to know about running a business is that you have to throw any sense of humbleness right out the door. Brag to everyone about how wonderful your shop is, how they don't want to miss a single bit of it. Are you planning a real grand opening, I hope?" Frannie sniffs. "Soft openings are a waste of time, as far as I'm concerned."

"Actually, yes. That's why my goal is to open by Small Business Saturday." The Saturday after Thanksgiving, after Black Friday, seemed perfect when I was writing in my planner last June. Now, only a couple weeks out, it looks insane.

"I suppose that's a good time to launch a Christmas

shop. I mean, it sounds like you'll have to count on your seasonal revenue to carry you for the rest of the year?" Her pained expression tugs at my *will-I-fail?* anxiety.

"Oh, it's not a Christmas shop. Christmas will be twenty-five to sixty percent of my stock, depending upon the time of year. I'm carrying items for every imaginable holiday around the world. And lots of fun gift items. Don't worry, I'll keep both the tourists and locals happy with my selections." I don't like that I'm feeling defensive about something I've planned in so much detail. But Frannie doesn't know the kind of work I did in the Navy, that launching a business feels second nature after following flight checklists before and after every mission. Except for this part. Tiptoeing around the locals. Because I won't be moving in two years, I won't be able to start over like I did with each new duty station. Putting down roots has its risks, too.

Frannie's perfectly groomed brows arch above her trendy frames. "Really? That's far more ambitious than I realized. Make sure I get a grand opening poster for my office window."

"Poster?" My stomach sinks as I realize I haven't even begun to think about print promotion. I've been so wrapped up in getting the inventory ready for retail, both physical and via the website. Social media is where I've put all my promo eggs. I never considered the good, old-fashioned tried and true. My palm itches to slap my forehead.

Frannie's expression softens, and compassion glimmers

in her eyes. She reaches across the expansive desk and puts her hand on my forearm.

"Don't stress. Groundhog Quick Print over on Loganberry Drive does a wonderful job. They'll give you a local business discount and do the design work, too. Tell them I sent you."

"Thanks for the info, Frannie. I'll stop in there on Monday." I mean it. Frannie interpreted my silence correctly and offered an immediate, viable solution. The spiky hot caterpillars in my gut turn to warm butterflies of gratitude. They remind me I've made the right decision to start over in Stonebridge.

"One Way or Another" sounds from Frannie's designer bag and she retrieves her phone, removes her sunglasses and perches a pair of red-framed reading glasses on her nose. She reads the Caller ID and frowns, then holds the phone to her ear.

"Jenna. Where are you?" Frannie's tone turns sour on a dime, and I inwardly cringe. I'd witnessed how Frannie runs her office with an iron fist. I've been there. I'm constantly reminding myself that not everyone has had the benefit of quality leadership training. Let's just say I'd never talk to a subordinate with such a tone of disdain, at least not in public, even on the phone.

"Let me guess, he's too busy to get it himself?" Frannie actually *tsks* her disapproval. "Go ahead, get his coffee, then go back and get my usual. I'll text you where and when to bring it. Ken will have to rely on himself for his showing this afternoon. I need you more than he does." Frannie's tone is so caustic, a complete one hundred and eighty degrees out from the sunny tone she took with me. Is her head going to start spinning?

Frannie turns her attention back to me and lowers her reading glasses. She winks. "See what I mean about the perils of running your own business? Jenna comes off as a sweet young woman, but she's human. Give her a five-minute break and she takes half an hour. I've learned over the years to always make it clear that I'm the boss. Remember, Angel. You can't please everyone."

"Um, thanks." Explaining to Frannie that I have two decades of leadership experience isn't an option, and not only because it'd be a pure ego exercise on my part. Frannie's not a listener.

"Tell Quick Print that I sent you. Their website is fun, with an easy graphic design app that you can fiddle with until they open on Monday."

"Will do." I check my phone for the time. "Look, Frannie, I hate to rush you—"

"Say no more!"

"It's just that I already had an appointment to get coffee at Latte Love."

"Oooh, fun! I rarely get to actually sit and chat in there, I'm always on the run. Are you meeting someone?"

"Yes. My sister. Crystal?"

"Oh."

Frannie's brows raise, and her lips purse as if something important has occurred to her. Or maybe she's trying to place Crystal. It's not as though their paths cross much—Crystal and her husband have been in the same house for thirty years. I'm about to ask Frannie about it when she returns to her happy self and nods, pats me on the forearm again.

"Wonderful. You must be so happy to be back with family." She looks at her phone. "Oh boy. I've lost track of time myself. I'm so sorry but I have to jaunt off to a showing. You've got my number—let's get together!"

We loosely hug—the Stonebridge version of a wave—and I walk her through the front of the shop and let her out the front door. I expect her to head toward her office, with the black-and-white striped awning, visible several blocks down. Instead she turns to the right, toward the end of town. She's probably got her own property showing on schedule.

Schrock Real Estate has blossomed over the years. Frannie and Ken have a lot to be proud of. Their signs are in front of the vast majority of sale properties in Stonebridge, and real estate has seen an uptick as young couples are flocking to more suburban, semi-rural settings after making their mark in any one of the major cities that surround us. Besides Philly and Pittsburgh, we're only two hours from Washington, DC, and three from New York. Frannie and Ken made my property purchase easier than it might have been, via their junior agent Dave, working with me across the miles to get the myriad documents signed. I literally walked into the title company's office on a quick trip from Belgium last December and closed on the building in under two hours. This allowed for the extensive amount of rehab that was needed to be done before the girls and I ever rolled into town. As I told Frannie, we'd finished the rest of the re-do this past summer.

There's no doubt that Schrock Real Estate is a success. Frannie and Ken are living the American dream. Yet I don't get the feeling that Frannie thinks she has that much to be happy about. If her tone with Jenna is any indication, I suspect their office environment remains intense. Whenever I've been in their office, I'm usually yukking it up with Ken, who ran cross-country all four years of high school, same as me. Ken and I were closer friends than Frannie and I, back in the day.

I'm going to be late for coffee with Crystal if I don't hurry, so I quickly make sure Ralph's locked in his cage, still in front of the large store window. I shove my arms into a red wool coat and twist a sparkling silver hand-knit scarf from Bryce around my neck. The hand-painted Russian broach I've pinned to my lapel dresses up my otherwise casual attire. The intricate design features a couple in a troika, with tiny snowflakes dusting the scene.

Ralph gives me a side-eye from his heated perch.

"See you later, sweetie." I say.

"Bye-bye." He mimics the twins, who have the same pitch, in his usual sad voice. I ignore the tug at my heartstrings. He'll be fine for the few hours I'll be gone.

Within five minutes I'm at Latte Love, invigorated by the cold gusts of wind that hastened my pace. I'm never not impressed by the gray-stone building that used to be the town jail, then fifty years later, the police station. It became a coffee shop several years back, but changed owners more than once from what I've heard. I'm not going out on a limb to say Latte Love is located in Stonebridge's most sturdy edifice.

"Hey," Crystal greets me through the open passenger window of her white Jeep. I blink. I didn't see her pull up.

"Hi!" I wave. While I wait for her to parallel park, I make a mental note to ask her about Frannie and Ken. And realize that not only did Frannie not answer my question about how Ken was, she barely mentioned him, save for dissing him in front of her employee. And me.

I'm aware that as a widow, it's easy for me to put Tom on a pedestal, but the truth is that he was the love of my life. Is Ken still Frannie's soul mate? Or is something going on I'm unaware of?

Crystal and I hug, then walk up the stone steps of Latte Love together. Finally, the day turns to what I came back home for. Normalcy.

Chapter Four

"I'M NOT SURPRISED she didn't bring up Ken." Crystal shoves her John Lennon glasses up the bridge of her nose. We're seated at a back-corner booth, perfect for two. "They almost lost the business because of his tomfoolery. And now there are rumors that she's running around on him."

"*Tomfoolery? Running around?*" I try not to laugh. In the Navy, it'd be described as *dicking around*, or, when it was a guy who'd messed up, it was said he'd *stepped on it*. As in, he'd stomped on his own private parts.

"Infidelity is not funny." Crystal sets her cup down. Her simple drink, a cappuccino, was ready ahead of mine, a fancier choice from Latte Love's creative menu. "You know the beginnings of their story. They married young and finished college early to make a life for their son."

"Right. They both went to HACC and finished there, right?" I'm referring to Harrisburg Area Community College. "Frannie mentioned their son's doing well in the Marine Corps."

"That's always good to hear. But after he left home,

Frannie went through a meltdown. She was depressed if you ask me, and neglected herself along with their marriage. Ken strayed. The town figured it out and tongues wagged, as they do. But then, they supposedly patched things up."

"Elf latte for Angel!" The barista calls out my order. I grin at Crystal and hold up my index finger. "Hold that thought."

I slide out of the booth and walk around several seated customers, some solo, working on laptops, others engaged in animated conversation. The counter is empty save for a foot-tall silver tinsel Christmas tree festooned with iridescent twinkling lights, and my drink. The same young woman who took our order offers a smile.

"Thank you!" I grab the paper cup and reach for a lid. But when I see the intricate design sprinkled with pale green, gold and silver sugar atop the rich foam, I pause. Etched in the froth is an elf, a tiny red poinsettia flower hanging from its hat. Latte art really is a thing.

"This is beautiful. I almost don't want to drink it. Thank you." No wonder my drink took longer than Crystal's.

The young woman looks over her shoulder, toward the back corner of the service area. "Nate did it."

I follow her gaze to what I expect will be another millennial, so it takes me a heartbeat or two to realize she's referring to the tall, attractive, silver-haired guy emptying roasted beans into one of two commercial grinders.

"Thanks, Nate!"

"Sure thing." He nods, continuing his work behind the counter.

I wait for him to look up, and when he does I raise my cup in thanks. And come scarily close to dumping the hot drink on myself when my sudden gasp makes my arm jerk.

Did I say Nate was an attractive older man? Strike that. He's a smokin' slice of silver foxdom. And not so old, not if you consider me "not" old. As in fortyish. Okay, I'm forty-five.

Nate is a nice surprise. Still, I pride myself on a key pilot lesson: Keep any distractions to a minimum.

And Nate is just that. A distraction. Or he would be if I was in the market. But dang, his eyes.

Cool your jets.

When I return to my seat, Crystal's lips are curled upward and her eyes sparkle with sisterly wisdom. "You haven't met Nate yet, huh? He's fairly new in town, since May. He's bought out the previous owner and doesn't sling coffee as much as he works behind the scenes." Wow. He beat me here by a month. I've been in Latte Love often but never noticed him. Has the shop taken so much of my focus that I overlooked Nate? No, there's no way any woman with a shred of libido would miss him.

"No, but I've met him now." I try to act disinterested as I stare at Nate's latte art, but the heat on my cheeks has to be visible to anyone within a mile radius. And I can never hide anything from my sister. "I don't remember him in school.

Do you?"

"Nate Silver. He's not from Stonebridge. He grew up in Lancaster and lived in New York City for years, meaning twenty plus. Word is that he's moved back to help his parents out. He's single and...wait for it...straight." Crystal giggles. If I'm not careful Crystal and my family will be trying to set me up with the intriguing coffee shop owner. I'm not against dating, per se, just not seeking it out. Not yet.

At least not until the shop's up and running.

Chicken.

"How do you know so much about him already?" I feel like a creep, talking about the nice man who made my coffee so pretty. I answer my own question in unison with Crystal.

"Bryce."

We burst out laughing. Of course our brother would be the one to find out all the deets on the new man. Bryce loves his husband, but remains an incurable flirt. Nico has the patience of...well, a man who knits for a living. Nico's the creative energy behind Skeins and Baahls while Bryce runs the business side of things.

Our laughter attracts several glances, and I wipe my eyes, take my first sip of the latte. As the almond-flavored foam chased by espresso with cocoa notes rolls over my tongue, I close my eyes and savor the combination.

"Stop fighting yourself, Angel." Crystal nods at my coffee. "Enjoy it." I know she's referring to more than the coffee, more than the latte art.

A sigh emerges from deep in my ribcage. "I'm not there yet, Sis." Although when I reach for that ache in my heart, the one Tom left behind, I find…warm memories. His smile. But not the urge to retreat into my grief as I did for a very long time.

"You won't be *there* until you make a move to be. It's been a long time, and the girls are gone most of the year now. You have your home, a new career, your own life to live. It's okay to at least think about putting yourself out there again. Tom wouldn't want anything different for you. Just sayin.'" Crystal does an impressive Gaelic shrug for having lived in Pennsylvania her entire life.

"Trust me, my days are full. I have a business to get off the ground, remember?"

"Of course! And I'm so excited for you and the shop. But whether it's flying Navy planes or stocking your store shelves, work can't be everything. I don't want you to be lonely. You deserve it all, Sis. You're still young, and you have so much love to give."

"That's what Ralph's for." I'm done with the self-examination. "Where were we? Oh yeah. Frannie and Ken." I raise my brow at my sister, in the way that never fails to make her giggle. Which she does, but quickly extinguishes her mirth as if the subject of Stonebridge's premier real estate pair is emotionally onerous.

"After their son left for the service, they had that huge

falling out. More like a fracture. She wasn't herself, frankly. Her sunny, positive nature seemed to dry up for a spell."

"That's not unusual for empty nest, though, is it?" Except for the public part, and I couldn't remember when Frannie and Ken had ever been private about anything when we were all teens. "They've always been who they are, open about their relationship and what they mean to one another. When kids leave…it's a stressful time." I'd had my share of melancholy since dropping the girls off at college two months ago. "If not for the shop and my deadline to open by the end of the month, I might have flipped out about now."

"You? No way. You're way too grounded. Too organized."

I grunt, knowing I don't have to remind Crystal about how scattered I was that first year, and occasionally since, after Tom died.

"*Grounded* is what I like to hear after all that time in the skies." I think about how things might have looked for Frannie and Ken when their son left. "Whether you have a business to run or not, though, it's still a major adjustment to let your kids go. It's important to have something new to focus on, no matter how small. Look at me—I'm knitting."

"Only because Bryce threatened to sibling-divorce you if you didn't learn. It's good for his business if you have a skein or two sitting on your counter, to point customers down to his shop." Crystal referred to how the yarn store was situated back from the main drag, in a former Victorian merchant home. It was perhaps the most delightful place in Stone-bridge, with seating areas in several rooms and a fully stocked coffee and tea station free to all knitters.

"Yet they do as well as any of us on Main Street."

"True, but trust me, Angel, I know how Bryce thinks every other business in town is related to Skeins and Baahls. He convinced me to do a floral arrangement with his fluffiest Angora yarn. Handmade knitting needles with glass marbles on top included." She grins and shakes her head. "As for Frannie and Ken, they did try to do new things after they patched things back up. Or at least, Ken did. He started golfing regularly, more than he had as a real estate agent. Dad sees him out on the course, and they've played together several times. Frannie, though, can't seem to do anything but work. She's channeled her energies toward expanding the business and she hasn't stopped."

"So what's the problem now? Between her and Ken?" I honestly hadn't seen one iota of trouble between them until this morning when Frannie spoke to her assistant so disparagingly about Ken.

"She's tightened up on all their rental properties over the past couple of years. Raised the rents, started kicking out folks for the most minor infractions. Residential and commercial alike. No one escapes her wrath." A chill runs down my spine. Crystal tilts her head.

"What?"

"I didn't tell you how Frannie stopped by earlier. She

tried to knock on the shop's main entrance, but when I didn't answer, she came around the back. I opened the door, but she was in the middle of doing it herself. She had a key."

Crystal's eyes bulge like the Grinch's dog when the Grinch halters him. "You've got to be kidding me. That's awfully bold. But wait—you mean you haven't changed the locks?"

"No. My bad."

Crystal leans in. "Remember the Tasty Tea?"

"Of course." Images of three-layer coronation chicken salad sandwiches on pristine white bread, currant mini scones, and ivory petit fours with silver dragées flooded my mind. We've had Christmas tea there with our Mom several times. "I thought it closed because Sylvia Radabaugh decided to retire?"

"She'd hoped to keep it open, under new management by her niece and goddaughter, once she semi-retired to Rehoboth Beach. She tried to purchase the building outright, but Frannie wouldn't budge on her over-the-top price and also refused to lower the inflated rent. To top it off, Frannie insisted it was her right to enter at any time, which as the building owner of course she did, but still. Sylvia had run the shop for decades. Frannie treated her like she was a fly-by-night. Sylvia complained about the way Frannie would let herself in and snoop around the place. The straw that broke it all up was when an anonymous tip about rodent infestation was reported to the Department of Health. Because of the fines and extermination costs Sylvia had no choice but to close up shop. The building's still empty, by the way."

"Wait—are you saying Frannie deliberately put mice in Sylvia's tea shop?"

"Oh no, not at all. Rats. She put rats in there." An image of a rat scurrying up a ship's line from land flashes in my mind. The only thing that stopped it was the rat guard, hung strategically on the steel rope. The only rat guard that will help me ashore in Stonebridge is to change my dang locks.

"Was there any proof of this?" It's hard to believe Frannie has sunk so low.

Crystal sighs. "Do you need proof? I don't. Neither does any business owner on Main Street. Not after watching Frannie's behavior the last year. It's like she doesn't care about Schrock Real Estate's reputation anymore. She and Ken barely speak to one another in public, it has to be frosty at their house in the hills. My best guess is that she's in it for a money grab before they divorce."

"That is unfortunate. What did Sylvia's niece end up doing?"

Crystal nods toward the coffee counter, where the young woman who served us wipes down the surface, straightened the various types of creamers. "That's her—Amy Radabaugh. She's going to graduate school while she works hourly here."

"Well, I'm sorry it didn't work out, but—"

"Amy had counted on the job to pay for her living expenses while she earned her MBA. More importantly, it was a family business, meant to be passed on. A legacy."

"I'm surprised Sylvia didn't own the building." But I also know it's not always feasible for a small business owner to own their commercial venue. It's a reminder that I'm one of the lucky ones.

"Sylvia's not the only business owner affected by the Schrock's hardline. As various commercial sites came up for sale, Frannie and Ken bought them up. Not unexpected for a successful real estate business, but when word got out that they were buying buildings and then raising rents, forcing long-time renters out, it didn't go over well."

"Sounds like Monopoly." I never liked board games. Give me tag Frisbee any day.

"Some folks say it's good to clean up our downtown, maybe bring it into the twenty-first century. To be fair, their tactics got rid of a few eyesores. And brought in others." Crystal smirks but on her it's cute, like one of Santa's elves.

"Such as the new apartment building going up?" I'm referring to where ground's broken on what, from the architectural drawings posted at the construction site, reminds me of a European galleria of sorts. Beautiful in Naples, Italy, but out of place in Stonebridge, PA. "That looks awful, to be fair. I'm surprised that the town council allowed it."

"Sweetie, Frannie *is* the town council, the Stonebridge Historical Guild, the Citizens for Stonebridge, the Stonebridge Small Business Buddies. Learn that or perish in this town."

Crystal can be dramatic, but there's nothing hyperbolic in her tone. Her warning is the real deal, as is her next question.

"Please tell me you've joined to the Stonebridge Buddies."

Chapter Five

"**Y**OU HAVEN'T BEEN to any one of the Buddies meetings yet, have you?" Crystal's accusation hits hard.

Heat flushes my face, and I fight my defensiveness. Crystal, like any trusted sister, can smell my discomfort a mile away and isn't above using it to make me comply with her vision of how my life should be. All with the most loving motives, of course.

"I'm too busy right now. Besides, I'm fortunate that I own my building. Other than dictating what kind of potted plants and sidewalk signs I can have, what kind of power does Frannie have over me, really? Not to mention, Frannie is my friend. *Our* friend." Even though Frannie had shown no sign of remembering Crystal earlier.

"Listen to me, Angel. A high school friend, unless you've closely kept up with them, is an acquaintance, nothing more. Best you remember that, as you go forward."

Crystal isn't being a jerk, or patronizing. At least not willfully, or in a mean way. She's my big sis and has always looked out for me. And as much as I have zero problem matching her stubbornness with mine, Crystal is usually right.

"There are more small-town rules than there are Navy flight regulations."

I stare at my sister, overwhelmed by all I need to catch up on. Between not living here for so long and being immersed in creating a new life and business since our move-in five months ago, I'm woefully behind on Stonebridge's happenings.

"Who knows? Now, on to more important stuff. How are my beautiful nieces doing?" Crystal's eyes light up as if we're discussing her favorite thing in the world. Which we are, save for her family, which consists of her, her husband, and my nephew Joey. She's been the auntie Ava and Lily can rely on through thick and thin. Trust me, there's been a lot of thin from the twins losing their father way too soon, to my mercurial moods. Not to mention the constant state of transition military life imparted. No matter what, though, Aunt Crystal has been their bestie, sounding board, and brilliant mentor.

"The girls are fantastic. Ava's thrilled with both of her roommates, Lily has one that's a jerk. I'll find out more tomorrow when we have our group video chat." A sudden, sharp yearning for my girls stabs me in the heart. I blink, fighting the tears. Crystal says nothing but reaches out and gives my hand a quick squeeze. I'm glad she doesn't push for more info, doesn't say anything about how quickly they grew up. Public crying isn't my gig.

Comfortable silence settles between us, and we take our time finishing our drinks.

"What are you going to do for the rest of the day?" Crystal asks.

"What am I *not* going to do?" I grin, and tell her about the damaged stock, how excited I am to see glimpses of the finished shop among the messed-up shelving. And secretly wonder if my idea of a life change is too much. Maybe Tom's idea to launch a local flight school would have been wiser.

But Crystal soon has me back onto a positive vibe, and I'm more determined than ever to make Shop 'Round the World a success. I'm being silly, letting a few surprises unsettle me.

When has the unknown ever kept me from going for it?

BY THE TIME I finished coffee with Crystal, grabbed a quick lunch at a local sandwich place and ran several more errands, it was almost time for the Saturday afternoon Mass at Saint Josephine's, so I opted to swing by church and leave myself all of Sunday to work in the shop, uninterrupted. I'm not a hardline Catholic, by any means, but I've found comfort in the familiar since returning home. And it makes me get out of the house, away from work for a bit. Since the girls left it's all too easy to spend long days in the single building that is home and work for me.

I'm out of Mass in under an hour, thanks to Father Drew's most excellent seven-minute homily. I wasn't looking to rush through the service, but I'm beyond eager to get back to the shop.

Still, as I leave I make my way to the narthex where parishioners shake the priest's hand in greeting. I always say hello to Drew Griffin, now Reverend Drew. Or, more usually, Father Drew. But I still think of him as more friend than confessor. Drew and I went through grade school together until ninth grade, when I went to Stonebridge High and he attended Our Lady Help of Christians High School. We were buddies as young kids and that sense of connection has never faded, for which I'm grateful. He's surrounded by a gaggle of blue-haired women so I do a quick finger-wiggle wave, hoping to slide by.

"Angel, great to see you!" His enthusiastic greeting isn't something I can ignore so I reach out a hand to shake his.

"Hi, Father Drew." I call him by the moniker in public; it's only right and respectful. But to me, he'll always be the kid who liked to eat white craft paste in second grade. Sometimes mixed with tempera paint.

"We have to grab a cup of tea sometime." Father Drew's become an exclusive tea drinker, according to my mother, who organizes food for the rectory from time to time. She and Dad have Father Drew over for dinner every so often. It could be the coffee talk with Crystal, but I'm again hit by how tightly intertwined Stonebridge is, especially after coming from such a large duty station as NATO, Belgium.

"Absolutely. As soon as I get the shop up and running, let's do it!" I'll bring him a tea set from my Japanese merchandise that I think he'll like. It's sincere in that I'm happy to reconnect with a lifelong acquaintance, but I also know that Father Drew likes to counsel parishioners over a cup of green or black. Gifting him a nice tea service is the closest I'm going to come to doing any service for my church for now, what with the demands of Shop 'Round the World.

"I look forward to it. God Bless." Father Drew turns to a little girl who's tugging on his alb, grinning wide to show him where she lost her two front teeth.

I ease away from the crowd and hightail it back to the shop. I made a fair dent earlier, but I'd really like to have a clean slate for tomorrow. With the construction crew due back at seven A.M. on Monday, it'll be my last bit of quiet until the store's renovation is finished.

When I unlock the front shop door, Ralph flaps his wings from his heated perch. Lily and Ava did research on psittacines when we adopted him and insisted it would prevent arthritic claws in later parrot life. He's in the cage where I left him, but instead of waking from a nap, he's shaking with angst.

"*Eeeeetch*!" His screech makes my stomach plummet. More than any rough helo ride.

Something is very wrong.

Chapter Six

"HI RALPH. BUDDY. It's okay, Mommy's home. What's wrong? What are you saying, honey?" I have to stay calm for my feathered friend.

"*Eeetch*!" He makes the same hair-raising sound, and I've no idea what has my green chicken so stirred up. It's a new sound from him. It's normal for Ralph to greet me with a "hello," or "mommy's home," followed by a wolf whistle. All of which he learned since we adopted him from the avian rescue in Hawaii. And it's not unusual for Ralph to pick up new words and phrases from his favorite cartoon show. He knows all the words to the theme song, sometimes to my regret when he's on the umpteenth rendition in the same hour.

But there's no television in the shop, and I've never seen Ralph behave this way before. Ever.

"What, bud?" I open the cage door and he shrinks from me as if I'm sticking a snake inside instead of offering my finger. My stomach has moved on from its ten-story drop to whole-hearted flipping.

Breathe. Ralph's supposed to mirror my emotions, not

the other way around.

"It's okay, Ralph. Look, I'm sorry I was gone for so long. I only meant for it to be an hour, but I had to see Crystal and then I ran into Father Drew." I keep my tone soft, neutral. It appears to calm him, and I turn toward the back, hoping he takes a cue from my usual behavior and lets himself out. I cross my fingers that he'll relax enough to climb out to sit on the cage top perch.

I can't rule out a trip to the emergency vet, though. Birds go downhill quickly; by the time they're showing signs of illness it's often too late. I frantically scan my memory for where I put the information for the veterinarian and remember it's on a magnet on the side of the kitchen refrigerator. I need to put another one in my office.

Please, please let it be nothing.

"*Eeetch*!" Ralph tries to make me stay within eyesight, using his new—and beyond grating—sound to hold my attention.

"Gosh darn it, buddy, you're going to split my eardrums!" I shoot my reply over my left shoulder, still moving forward through the retail area. Birds aren't immune to separation anxiety, just like dogs and cats, so our family was extra careful to not reinforce any bad habits when we adopted Ralph. No big deal was made at good-byes or returns. We tried to keep things as status quo as possible, considering we were a Navy family.

But now, these past five months, we've had the most stable time our family has known since…forever. Save for the girls leaving, but my point is that Ralph's been in the same house, same place, for almost half a year. And we're settled, with no future moves in sight. So there's nothing that should be stressing Ralph out this much. Unless it's being in the shop alone that's spooked him? Or maybe he saw something he didn't like out on the street, through the window. I usually take him up to our living quarters instead of leaving him here in the store while I'm out.

It's okay. It's the new environment, is all.

Plus I was gone a lot today, for me. Coffee in the form of hours with Crystal and then Mass. The poor birdie got lonely. Relief at the logical explanation eases my tight shoulder muscles, and I continue toward the back rooms.

My gaze locks onto the hip-high mound of packing material piled in the center of the hallway. Motion eases stress so I start shoving the crumpled paper into an empty box, making quick work of the huge mound. As I reach for the last large clump of paper packing, I see the carton I threw the damaged merchandise into last night. My heart stills. The throwaway box is in front of me, in the hallway, a full six feet from the back door where I left it. Worse, it's not as full as I left it. All that remains in the battered box is one half of a Santa, two empty root beer bottles, and several chards of the former swizzle sticks. I know I threw both Santa halves in there, as well as larger portions of broken swizzle sticks.

My stomach dipsy-dives for the tenth time in three

minutes.

Dropping the paper, I pick up the box and shake it, as if maybe my eyes are deceiving me and the other tchotchke bits I'm certain I tossed in there will appear, hidden by a flap of cardboard.

Nope. Half a Santa figurine and the longest remains of red-and-green glass stirrers are gone. I know rodents can be an issue near commercial businesses, but I haven't had one sign of mouse or rat habitation in or near the building. Besides, they don't eat glass, do they?

"*Eeetch*!"

"Aaaah!"

It takes me a split second to realize that I screamed. I drop the box as if it's electrified.

Enough.

I'm letting my cold-case binge-TV mind affect my common sense. I shove the box aside with my foot, determined to finish clearing the packing debris. But when I lift the last bit of bubble wrap, I see a glove. A very familiar leather glove that matches a pair of expensive leather boots.

Ginger leather.

"What on earth?"

My heart stops for a full second before it *thumps* into overdrive.

A woman's glove with tiny amber seed buttons lies flat on the threshold between the hallway and storage room. I swear the hardwood floor waves under me as I pick up the glove and stare at it. This wasn't here earlier. I saw Frannie put both gloves on before she went out the door.

My sense of all I know, everyone I trust, warps, cracks, vibrates in anticipation of a total explosion.

It, it can't be—*no*. Absolutely not. I'm hot and cold at the same time, a trickle of sweat snakes down my spine. Oh, no, am I going to find a rat in the storage room? At my cherished beverage counter?

I spin around, look at the plate of cookies next to the sugar and tea bags. Nothing's disturbed.

No, this can't be what it looks like. It. Can't. Frannie wouldn't have come back in here without telling me. She might be a hard taskmaster to her employees, and she's definitely a cutthroat businessperson. She's not a breaking-and-entering type of gal, not after I caught her with the key earlier.

But...

Frannie's gloves were the same color as the one I'm holding, and have the same exact bead pattern. So she stopped in again when I wasn't here. But why? She gave me the tourism brochures. There was no reason for her to come back in. Rage snakes through me, smothers my fear of rodents.

I flip on the light switch to the storage room and face the skinny passage between the rows of neatly stacked boxes. Two boxes now lay in the path I've been fastidious about keeping clear. As if someone knocked them down.

Frannie or whomever, it doesn't matter. Someone's been

here without my permission.

Fear rushes back over me, freezing me in place. It's as if I'm in aviator swim qualifications again, my strokes meaningless against the rotor-wash kicked up by the helicopter that's lowered a line to rescue me. I have to push through this horrible inertia, figure out what's going on. But I sure as heck don't want to. My mind struggles with my frozen limbs. Training ingrained into me since my Naval Academy Plebe Summer is all that moves me deeper into the storage room when my entire being is screaming at me.

Get. Out.

I force my feet to move, to step over each box. I'm almost there, to where there's another clearing amidst the boxes I've already unpacked, in front of the deep shelves. My foot catches on something, sends a wash of horror up my leg as, at some level, I recognize what I've hit.

Don't look don't look…I look down.

The boot that matches the glove lies against the toe of my scuffed boot, the spicy color underscoring its owner's exquisite taste. The boot is on a very still, unmoving, foot. My gaze instinctively travels up from the boot, to the corduroy pants. *No, no, no*…

I home in on the face.

Frannie.

But not like I've ever seen her before. Shudders emanate from my center, my thoughts crash into one another.

I'm certain she's gone. As in dead. Deceased.

I've been in combat zones, and I've seen horrific things. Including dead bodies. So there's no doubt in my mind Frannie's soul has departed God's green earth. Tremors continue to rack my body as gooseflesh covers me. To make certain that I haven't lost it, that this really is a dead body, Frannie's body, I force myself to look again.

There's something protruding from her chest, the unmistakable dark stain of blood soaked into Frannie's fine cashmere pullover.

Check her pulse.

The voice of the Marine drill sergeant during basic first aid training in flight school takes over.

Administer CPR immediately.

I kneel down and find her wrist, press my fingers against it. Nothing. But the wrist isn't always a reliable pulse point. I lean over, touch the side of her neck. Her flesh is cool. As I feared, there's no pulse here, either. I stare at Frannie's unseeing eyes. Eyes with—*gulp*—my broken swizzle sticks stuck in them.

Who would do this? How can this be? I just spoke to her! Myriad thoughts assault my mind, keep me stuck in a whirlwind of disbelief.

Call 911.

"*Eeetch!*" Ralph's screech claws at my awareness and makes me jump. I bonk my head on the shelf above Frannie, and in one horrifying second two things happen. I identify the object in Frannie's chest. It's the broken Santa, the one I threw out yesterday. I'm also convinced I'm going to fall on top of her—her *corpse*—and I suck in a breath, scared witless. Lucky for me, I was born with a hard head and the momentum from it connecting with solid wood forces me backward, and I land on my butt.

The pain that shoots through my tailbone grounds me, shakes me out of my shock. I take huge gulps of air, praying the rush of oxygen to my brain will enable me to focus. To do the right thing by Frannie in the middle of my freak-out.

What's shaking me to the depths of my soul isn't that there's a dead body in my shop. It's that it's Frannie, the grade school friend I memorized multiplication tables with, her Latte Love cup still clutched in her gloved left hand, her nutmeg shade of lipstick imprinted on the cup's white lid. And she's been brutally murdered. The sight of two of *my* broken swizzle sticks—one striped red and white, and one white swirled with green—in her eyeballs, and one of *my* Santa statues in her chest, makes this personal.

Not only did someone kill Frannie, they used my damaged merchandise to do it.

My knees and legs are shaking too much to trust them so I crawl out of the space, to the well-lighted hallway. As soon as I'm out of the storage room, I take my phone out of my back pocket and dial 911.

"911, what's your emergency?"

I start sobbing uncontrollably. I've had to report ugly things in my twenty-three-year military career. But I've never uttered the words that will be burned into my brain forever.

"There's a dead body in my shop."

Chapter Seven

"WHAT TIME DID you leave for Latte Love?" Detective Trinity Colson's brows remain straight and unmoving as she watches me with her bright brown eyes, as observant as they've always been. We were best friends since first grade and all through high school, but I've never seen this side of her. The "I think you might have killed a woman" side.

"I told the rookie, I mean, Officer Sam. His name is Sam McCloud, right?" I look at my childhood bestie, hoping for a bone. "I left my shop right after Frannie left, sometime around ten-thirty. I came back here later in the afternoon after I left church. I went to the four o'clock Mass."

"Did anyone you know see you there?" Some distant part of my mind understands what Trinity's doing, that it's part of her job, not personal. But having someone who once knew me so well question my truth makes me shake more.

"Father Drew. The parishioners who were in the back, when I left."

"Names?"

"I, I don't know."

Trinity sighs, making a single dark curl on her forehead dance. We're still in my office, where she's been questioning me for the last hour. The Stonebridge PD forensics team, a.k.a. four officers trained specifically for this purpose, are working the scene in the storage room. I notice they're taking all kinds of samples from the room, as well as going into the front retail area. I warned them not to stick their fingers in Ralph's cage. He's unpredictable when stressed, and since he's so good at picking up on my mood, I'd say he's mere heartbeats from stroking out. At least, that's how I've felt since finding Frannie.

The image of her too-still body defiled with what are supposed to be festive decorations is permanently scored into my memory.

Sitting here with Trinity allows me the chance to check out my office, which I bypassed when I was following the trail to Frannie. My stomach sinks at the overturned desk drawers that were thrown against the wall, their contents strewn everywhere. I haven't had a chance to see if anything's been taken yet. I didn't have any valuables in the desk, so it's not a priority but I can't help wondering what the murderer was looking for. Or if they had an accomplice who searched my desk while they killed Frannie.

A burnt-orange wool coat—Frannie's—is strewn over a column of stacking boxes meant for the window display and reminds me of a flag. A sign. It wasn't tossed there casually as the bandboxes would have been knocked down. Someone placed her coat there deliberately.

In short, Frannie's murderer wants to frame me. Or maybe the murderer was here to rifle through my stuff and happened upon Frannie? But again, why was Frannie back here in the first place?

I'm both exhausted and wired. My mind is fried. I need my sister, my brother, my family, but I haven't been allowed to call anyone yet. Trinity hasn't accused me of murder, and I want to believe she realizes I'd never do something so macabre. But…yeah. There's a dead body in my new shop, and it appears my damaged stock was the murder weapon.

Nausea rises, not for the first time, and I close my eyes, take a tiny sip of water. I got both of us a bottle from the small refrigerator in my office when Trinity first arrived. When I had no doubt she'd believe me.

"You're awfully interested in Officer McCloud's reaction, Angel."

"Well, he did puke up whatever he had for lunch all over my floor." I hear how shallow it sounds and grimace.

"It's upsetting for anyone to see such a grisly crime. McCloud's definitely a rookie but he knows how to do his job." I'm not surprised she's defending her officer. I'd expect no less. But she's treating me like I had something to do with this, and it's the last thing I need right about now. "I have to ask you all the questions again, Angel."

"Because Frannie was murdered."

"You're certain it was a murder?" Trinity didn't add

"which makes you my number one suspect." She doesn't have to.

"Of course I think it's, it was, a murder." I hope I sound more confident than I feel. "I don't have the law enforcement experience, you're the expert. But I'm sorry, a dead body with a Santa statue stabbed through the heart and swizzle sticks poked in the eyeballs like olives in a dry martini? Call me an armchair detective, but that's not any kind of natural death."

"Don't sell yourself short. Maybe you should have applied to SPD instead of opening up your own shop." She gulps from her bottle of water. Keeps her gaze on me. Doesn't lift her mouth in that quirky grin that always made me giggle back in the day. No, Trinity's all about being the successful Stonebridge PD detective that she is. I search my memory for what my Mom's told me about Trinity over the years. She was a cop in Harrisburg for many years, which is part of why we lost touch. The other reason is the Navy. Regret at the lost connection wells, and I shove it back. I can't fix the past.

Trinity takes a phone call but doesn't move from her seat, doesn't take her gaze off me. I'm frantic to read her mind. I have to know she doesn't *really* think I did it. As soon as she ends the conversation, I go for it.

"Who would do this, Trinity? And why here?"

Trinity's eyes narrow, and her professional demeanor never slips. "I can't talk to you about it, Angel. Just answer my questions."

"Okay." I let out a breath, nod. "I get it." I've been in-volved in my share of Navy investigations. And I want Trinity to know I'm a professional; I won't press her for more information. But it doesn't mean I can't try to figure some things out myself, does it?

Unless she locks you up. She wouldn't lock me up, would she?

"You know I didn't do this, don't you?" The question spills out of me like Frannie's coffee did this afternoon. I'm praying for Trinity's affirmation. That she absolutely knows, beyond a shadow of a doubt, that I didn't commit this horrible crime. Murder.

"I'm going to need a list of everyone who's come into your shop since you opened. And you're going to have to come down to the station to give an official statement." Nope, not Trinity's job to comfort me.

Stay strong.

"Of course. Whatever you need. For the record, I'm not open yet. It's in two weeks..." But will I still have a business to open, once word gets out that a random killer used my wares to off one of my high school classmates? "You don't really think I did it, do you, Trinity?" Again, the words seem to have a life of their own.

"This isn't about what I think, Angel. It's about the facts. A dead body is in your storeroom, with your products used as weapons. You say you didn't see or meet with Frannie anytime in the last twenty-four hours, besides earlier today?" She's tapping on her tablet, and I'd be impressed by how she slips in the scary question if I wasn't worried about ending up in the brig.

"No, I haven't seen her except in passing." Back when I'd blithely strolled Main Street, thrilled to be back in Pennsylvania. When Stonebridge still promised me nothing more than peace and healing. When I thought my days of deep tragedy were behind me.

Waves of panic choke me. I cough, try to make it seem as if I'm clearing my throat, not gasping for my sanity. I blink rapidly, not wanting to lose it in front of Trinity. We were very close at one point, and we've met for lunch twice since I've been back, but time will tell if we'll resurrect our once unbreakable bond.

Could Trinity even be my friend, now that I'm a murder suspect?

"We're going to have to sweep the entire shop, and your living quarters. It'll take tonight and tomorrow. Do you have a local place you can stay after you give your statement at the station?"

"Yes. My parents." I give her the address, then think better of it. They're out of town, and do I want to bring them into this any sooner than I need to? "No, wait—I'll stay with my brother. Mom and Dad are in Baltimore until tomorrow." Bryce will keep a calm head, and Nico knows how to dole out empathy like no other.

"Do you have any upcoming trips planned?"

"Um, no."

"I can't make you stay in town officially, but I'd like you to stick around, Angel." She conveys zero empathy as she draws her mouth into a grim line. I see tiny wrinkles around her lips. Did Trinity still smoke?

"So I'm a suspect?"

"Until I check your alibi, yes."

At Latte Love, I was seen not only by Crystal but Frannie's assistant Jenna, Amy Radabaugh, Sylvia's niece, and of course Nate the Silver Fox barista. Thank goodness Crystal and I spent almost three hours gabbing—it makes it certain that I couldn't have killed Frannie. Doesn't it? And then I went to afternoon Mass, where Father Tom saw me. Trinity will be able to clear me soon, I'm certain.

Guilt tugs at me. If I'd come back to the shop sooner, if I hadn't detoured to Mass, would I have been back in time to save Frannie? Would I have looked into the eyes of a cold-hearted killer?

"Gather your things. Officer McCloud will drive you to the station."

To their credit the police allow me to put Ralph upstairs, give him fresh food and water, and get my purse. But that's it. I'm quickly escorted out of my own home.

As I get into the back seat of the cruiser—a first for me— I try to ignore the searching gazes of the small crowd that's gathered beyond the crime scene tape. I don't let my thoughts wander to my girls, wondering if I'll miss their call tomorrow. And I force myself to not think about the obvious. That after years of honorable service to my country I've come back to what I thought was the safest place on the planet and become a murder suspect.

Chapter Eight

"**Y**OU'VE GOT TO be kidding. No way does Trinity think you did it. She wouldn't have let you go if she thought you were a cold-blooded murderer." Bryce shudders, never mind that he's wrapped in a moose-print faux-fur robe. He insists on behaving as if we live in Maine instead of a Mid-Atlantic state. His hip against his kitchen counter, he motions for me to down a shot of courage in the form of his own concoction of Irish cream whiskey. I throw it back, not in the mood to savor anything. He makes it special for the holidays, and I would normally have teased him about making it so early this year, but in the moment, I'm grateful for the burn down my throat.

"I'm telling you, you should have seen her face, Bryce. She is one hundred percent hardboiled detective." As I lick the thick liquor from my lips, the burn hits my gut and I'm reminded why I don't usually drink.

"She's Trinity, for goddess's sake. You've known each other for eons." Bryce isn't giving into what he sees as my trauma-drama addiction. To be fair, I was a bit of a brat as a kid and often used emotional manipulation to get my older siblings to do my will. But we're all in our forties and we're talking murder, not whether I can go to the movies with them.

"Don't mind him, Angel. Bryce is upset because one of our top suppliers told us today that they can't deliver in time for our trunk show. You can stay with us as long as you need, honey." Nico puts an arm around me and escorts me to where he's unfolded their sleeper sofa and made it up with blue-and-white snowflake flannel sheets. "Let Uncle Nico tuck you in."

"Thanks, but I think I'd better brush my teeth first." I sit on the mattress. "You two have to explain to me how someone would be angry enough to hurt, much less murder, Frannie. What on earth could she have ever done to warrant it?"

"Well…" Nico's face flushes. He hates confrontation, and I don't think I've ever heard him speak poorly about another person. "It's not for me to say—"

"So let me." Bryce plops down next to me, his heft launching me several inches into the air and heralding squeaks from the sofa bed frame that rival their Pomeranian's yipping. Purl, said dog, is curled up under a Rudolph throw on her princess bed—one of three—in the corner of the living room. "Frannie has done a clean sweep of Stonebridge, sister. Nary a friend was left when she got done trying to squeak every last penny from her renters and threatening business owners to participate in her schemes to put Stonebridge on the map or else."

"That's what Crystal said. Or else what?"

"Crystal didn't lie to you, Angel." His brows raise, and I notice the scruff on his generous chin. I realize I'm keeping them awake, and it's their busy season in the yarn shop.

But I have to figure some things out before I'll have a chance of getting any shut-eye. "What are you saying? That the murderer is one of what, thirty or so business owners in Stonebridge?"

"More like two hundred." Nico, the family's only CPA, speaks up from the Queen Anne chair where he's settled, a generous pour of the Irish cream liquor in the whiskey glass he's holding. "If you count all the commercial properties, insurance agents, real estate agents—there are agents besides the Schrock's—restaurants, the hair salons and barbershops, the storefronts downtown, it adds up. Don't forget, Stone-bridge's entire population passed fifteen thousand last census."

"Downtown proper is still level at fifteen hundred." Bryce adds.

"But Frannie doesn't, didn't, hold the lease on all of those commercial properties. Not by a long shot." Gratitude that I bought my building instead of leasing it makes my heart swell, until I remember it's moot. Frannie's not ever going to threaten my business.

"True, but it doesn't matter. She knew the ins and outs of local politics and red tape better than anyone. If you were on her good side, you got your building contract and permits in short order." Bryce winks at Nico. "Right, sweetheart?"

"Right." Nico shoots me an apologetic grin. "Frannie liked us because we had the money up-front when we purchased the store, and we paid cash for the house, too. Just like you did."

"So she had a good list and bad list." So where was I if she broke into the store?

"More like naughty and nice." Bryce says. "But even with us, she always tried to exert her will. She wanted to know how we were going to vote at the Buddies meetings, if we'd heard any dissention in the ranks."

"I'm need a list of who you think are Frannie's enemies."

"More like frenemies, you mean." Bryce pats my thigh. "In this town, no one is going to come right out and tell you they hate you. We're more *kill 'em with kindness* operators."

"Someone killed Frannie but it wasn't with any kindness."

THE NEXT MORNING the guys agree to let me pay for breakfast at the Sit Down Café, as a big thank-you for taking in a murder suspect. We have to get there by eight, because Stonebridge Skeins and Baahls opens at ten for a special trunk show of high-end yarn.

"Why did you two decide to open on a Sunday? You

swore when you quit your corporate jobs you'd never work weekends again."

"Except knitters love to get together on weekends. Saturday's our biggest revenue day." Bryce speaks with the same authority he had when running a Fortune 500 company's logistics for twenty years. Central Pennsylvania has been a commercial transportation hub since World War II, and attracts some of the world's largest distributors. Which explains why a small town like ours enjoys such a great economy.

Except Shop 'Round the World. How many businesses survive their first year? The daunting odds against me have been made exponential by the fact that Frannie was murdered there.

Before I can examine how cold-blooded my assessment is, Nico speaks. "Sunday was the only day we could get the designer in to Stonebridge. We're not DC or Philly, you know." He digs into his mile-high stack of cranberry pancakes while Bryce has already polished off most of his eggs Benedict. My veggie omelet sits untouched. The toast is all I've managed so far.

"If not for your slick talking we wouldn't have swung it, dear." Bryce sips his coffee. "Polly Pearlman is a hard cookie to grab."

"Hmm." I'm trying to stay in the moment, but, well, I found a body in my shop yesterday.

"Break out of it, Sis. It's all going to be okay. You're

okay. We're here." Bryce squeezes my shoulder. He has always been able to read my heart.

"Will it ever be okay again, though? A childhood friend, a stalwart—even if she's ticked off a lot of folks—member of the community, has been murdered. In my shop, before it's opened. And someone wanted it to look like I did it." I try to drink some tea but it only intensifies the roiling in my gut. Pulling out my phone, I look at Bryce and Nico, make sure they're paying attention. I don't want anyone to overhear.

"Quick, off the top of your head, give me the names of people and places you think have a grudge against Frannie." I open the Notes app on my phone.

"Well, there's Annie and Mel at the historical society." Nico says.

"Don't forget Ken, as in her widowed husband. Haven't seen them holding hands or giving one another so much as a wink in forever." Bryce frowns.

"Eloise." Nico swigs his coffee.

I stop. "Wait, what? Eloise the yoga instructor? My classmate?"

Nico nods. "I took her class for a few years. It wasn't good."

"Well, her yoga teaching was fine, dear." Bryce pats Nico's shoulder. "It was the other stuff."

"What other stuff?"

"She wanted to prove that the weirs were the source of some ancient chakra energy or some such."

"Weirs, as in the eel weirs that Mom is working with the Penn State researchers on?" An eel weir is a large, V-shaped formation of river rocks that indigenous peoples built in the Susquehanna river to capture eels. They are as wide as four football fields at their start, and narrow down to one point, where the fish are easily captured. Eels used to be plentiful in the Pennsylvania waters, including Jacob's Run, Stonebridge's Susquehanna tributary. A couple of years ago, a weir was discovered in Jacob's Run and had become a bone of contention with all interested local history buffs. Some believed, like Eloise and Mom, that the weir was indeed built by Natives, while most thought it was a mere replica, built by settlers and colonists in more recent centuries. Mom was heavily involved with the community volunteer team that worked alongside student and PhD archaeologists from the university.

It's hard to imagine now when fishing, canoeing, or rafting on the bucolic creek, but Jacob's Run used to be full of eels. An involuntary shudder runs down my spine. I've eaten all kinds of delicacies in my travels, but never acquired a taste for…eel. *Ick.*

"Eloise believes the weirs exist over eddies of energy, like the Red Rocks in Arizona." Nico's unaware of my gross-out thoughts and has that patient expression he's adopted over the years for whenever Bryce pulls b.s. out of thin air. "She could be right."

"Except Frannie didn't like Eloise's type of PR. She's

afraid, or, um, was afraid, that Eloise would draw in the van-living crowd, you know, trying to make Stonebridge a mini-Burning Man."

All I know about Burning Man is a documentary I watched with the girls last year. As part of the Navy, where everything is a team effort, it's not often that you get the opportunity to attend a self-reliance festival of any sort. Not that it doesn't intrigue me. But in Stonebridge?

"Wait, I thought Frannie was trying to grow the tourist population." And who would blame her for that? "That's a win-win for all of the businesses if you ask me."

"Frannie wants overnighters to stay in the hotel she and Ken invested in, not pitch camps and altars along Jacob's Run."

"Oh yeah. The Stonebridge Shoppe and Stoppe. I hate how she spelled it, by the way." The out-of-place glass galleria being built at the end of Main and Chestnut. The edifice that reminds me of Naples, Italy.

"That's the place. But don't say you hate anything about Frannie right now, dear. You know, being a suspect and all." Bryce's lips quiver as he represses a smile.

"The plaza's not finished yet. Why would she care about people who want to camp? They're two totally different crowds. Demographics. But they'll all spend money." I look at Nico, hoping he'll back me up, confirm my newbie business owner assessment.

"Frannie's not one to do anything halfway, Sis." Bryce

casts a critical eye on me, takes in that I'm taking notes on my phone. "When you asked for names last night, I thought you were still in shock. Why do you want to know all of this? Trinity knows this town backward and forward. What she doesn't know, she has people to provide the answers. You shouldn't get yourself involved in Frannie's murder any more than you are."

"You mean murder investigation. I'm not the murderer!" My voice comes out too loudly, and I slouch down on the booth seat. Too late. No less than three diners walk by, all taking time to look into our booth.

Nico waits for everyone to be out of earshot and clears his throat. "What he said. You're not in the Navy anymore, you don't have to solve every problem that crosses your desk."

"Or drops on your floor." Bryce deadpans.

"This is a lot more than a work problem for me. It's an everything problem. I can't go back to my own home, for heaven's sake!"

"Pshaw." Bryce shakes his head.

I stare at him. "Did you just say *pshaw*?"

"I did, and don't knock it. It's perfect for this conversation. Stay out of the investigation, Angel. You'll look guilty as all get out and tick off Trinity. Lose-lose, hear me?"

"I can't afford to stay out of it, Bryce. Nico, help me out here. You both know I'm opening in two weeks, and this entire case has to be history by then."

"I've read that some murder cases never get solved. Look at the poor woman who was murdered in Harrisburg in 1978—"

"Bryce." I grit my teeth. "I'm looking at Frannie Schrock's murder, which happened yesterday, in the building that houses my entire life!" My voice rises like an out-of-tune chorus belting out the last strains of "Silent Night" as my throat constricts. I don't dare take my stare off Bryce, because I know the entire restaurant heard me this time. I sense their censure, the shock of my selfish words.

In the Navy, every move I made was my superior's business, and I had to mind my manners 24/7. For good reason, don't get me wrong. But I made a commitment to myself and my family to begin a new life in Stonebridge. That means I need to care less about other people's opinions of me. I've got to find Frannie's killer and prove that Shop 'Round the World had nothing to do with her murder.

Which means I have to leave no clue unturned. If that means angering Trinity, then that's the price I'll pay.

Chapter Nine

A FTER BREAKFAST I walk down to my building only to find it swarming with police and other official-looking people who wear booties over their shoes and latex gloves to avoid leaving their prints on anything.

Trinity stops me at the front of the shop, the crisscrossing of yellow police that surrounds the building a sobering backdrop. "You can't go in yet."

I nod. My resolve to not care what Trinity thinks lessens as I meet the gaze of the woman who let me go last night, when we both know she could have taken me into custody. My prints are all over the murder weapons and the victim was in my shop. Damning circumstantial evidence at best, the lead-in to an indictment at worst.

"I can't promise, but it looks like we'll be wrapped up by the end of the day, definitely by tomorrow." Trinity stands with her hands on her hips, her police parka unzipped to reveal her V-neck charcoal pullover and burgundy collar blouse underneath.

"Aren't you cold, without gloves or a hat?"

"I've been running around all morning, so the cold air

actually feels good. Give me fifteen minutes, though, and I'll be looking for a hot cup of coffee."

"I can make you some in my office."

"Not right now, you can't." Her expression loses some of its edge. "This is more to protect you than anything, you know."

"Sure." I can't agree, but I don't want to tick her off. Not yet. There'll be plenty of time for that when she realizes I'm not waiting for her team to solve this. I'm going to dive in full throttle and do whatever I can do.

"You may as well go back to your brother's, or find somewhere else to hang for the rest of the day." Trinity's patience with my stalling is wearing thin if the downward curl of her mouth is a decent barometer.

"May I go upstairs, to get some fresh clothes? With an officer escort, of course. And I need to feed my bird."

"Ralph's fine. I, er, checked on him earlier." It's the first crack in Trinity's professional demeanor since yesterday. She met Ralph when I moved in this past summer, when she'd accepted my invitation to catch up over coffee. Turns out that Trinity had become a bird lover, too, and had two lovebirds, Malcolm and Harriet. She purses her lips. "Fine. Let me go with you."

I figure she's either taking pity on my circumstance, or she's following her nose. I took a shower at Bryce and Nico's, but having to put on the same clothes this morning, no matter that they were washed and dried by Nico, wasn't fun.

The stench of my stress sweat that permeates the sweater and jeans is beyond the powers of the most odor-neutralizing detergent.

Trinity walks under the crime scene tape and motions for me to follow, holding the tape up as I duck through. My gaze ping-pongs from one crime scene tech to another as we enter the shop through the front door and she leads me to the back stairwell, which allows me to see most of my office and storage room. I would have taken the home entrance to the left of the shop door, thinking I'm not allowed inside my shop while the cops are doing their jobs.

The store doesn't appear too messed up and the techs are leaving things be as much as possible. I try to focus on this, tell myself it'll be okay, I'll be able to continue with the shop.

And then I see the bright white tape, in the shape of a leg, on the storeroom floor. Dismay wells and smothers my tiny bit of hope. I freeze, unable to make my legs move, my stomach clenched in prep for a hurl.

No, no, no. I cannot lose it right here, right now. I've sucked down worse emotions in the past, haven't I?

You're a civilian now. Your friend was murdered.

I should know better. Didn't Tom's illness and death teach me that I have zero control over my emotions?

"You okay?" Trinity holds open the door to the stairs, waves me ahead.

I don't respond until we're in my kitchen, where I sink onto a chair and put my forehead on my arms. "I'm fine, I...

I…just…need a sec."

"Mommy's home!" Ralph's bright greeting doesn't give me the usual lift but instead triggers an intense longing for life before yesterday afternoon. Sobs wrench from deep inside, making my avoidance of the facts seem infantile. No matter that I know I'm innocent and I'm pretty certain Trinity knows this, too, the fact remains that I had the scare of my life yesterday. I could have gone to the clink or at least spent the night in a cell for something I didn't do. Which means my girls, Ralph, my entire family, could have been minus one. The thoughts tumble into a mess of illogic, and I can't do anything but keep my head down, suck in huge vats of air.

"Here." The sound of a glass on the wood table, the scrape of the chair legs as Trinity sits opposite me. I peek up and reach for the tall glass of water, suck it down in three full gulps. The nausea passes.

"I'm not giving you the best impression of myself, am I?"

Trinity's eyes are guarded, but there's a glimmer I know well. Compassion. "You can drop the tough girl charade with me, Angel."

"But you consider me a suspect."

"I had to, until proven otherwise." My ears perk at her use of the past tense. "We've confirmed your alibis and compared them with the coroner's estimated time of death. You're no longer a suspect."

"Even with my prints on the Santa stake and swizzle

sticks?" Does my mouth ever know when to stop?

"Yep. The prints were smudged, you know. The killer used gloves but wasn't that careful. He only cared about hiding their identity."

"'He?' Who do you think did this? And how in the world did one of my Santas do enough damage to kill Frannie?"

Trinity's mouth purses. "I shouldn't tell you, and you can't repeat this, but neither of your items led to her death. It was blunt force trauma to the back of her head."

"She was shoved? And hit one of the shelves." Oh no. It is my fault, no matter how indirectly. I had the contractor put in the strongest shelves possible. "If I'd picked a different style of shelf, or waited to install them—"

"That's the thing with a crime like this, Angel. You didn't know it was coming, couldn't have foreseen it. You're going to have a lot of similar thoughts over the next days and weeks as we get to the bottom of this. Whatever you do, do not blame yourself. Take it from me. Crime doesn't pay, and neither does misplaced guilt." Trinity's pretty face I remember from high school has transformed into a beautiful one, but I don't miss the extra life lines etched into her dark skin. I have them, too.

"I still can't believe you're a cop."

"Preach." She rolls her eyes. "Neither can my family. Dad's still asking if I'll ever consider law school at Dickinson, since it's so close." Dickinson Law School was in Carlisle, PA, only a half hour away.

"Would you?" I know my mid-life career change isn't unique.

"No way! I like working on catching the crooks. Let the lawyers and DA take care of the rest. My calling's on the streets."

"I suppose it's a long way from pre-law at Penn State, in your folks' eyes." Trinity, whose father was Black and her mother mixed Latinx and white, had disappointed her father when she hadn't chosen his alma mater. A Historically Black College and University, Howard was where he'd always hoped his children would go. Her mother wasn't so concerned about where her daughter enrolled and had been supportive of Trinity picking criminal justice for her undergrad major. But her mother had been horrified that her baby wanted to be a street cop instead of attorney.

"At least I'm back here in Stonebridge, closer to them. They do love their grandkids and now they get to see them almost every day." She'd worked in Harrisburg for fifteen years before transferring. Trinity's laugh brings a smile to my tired face. "My Dad is the best with the boys now, as a matter of fact. As hard as my teenage years were, he's made theirs bearable. Can you believe he taught them to fly fish? He finally got the sons he wanted."

"That's wonderful, Trinity. I hear you on the grandparent relationship. My parents are better with the twins than I am, lots of times. I suppose we'll do the same for our grand babies, someday."

Trinity regards me. "It's good to have you back, Angel. I haven't had a BFF in a long while." She quirks her mouth when she says *BFF*. Texting and clever acronyms weren't part of our adolescent lexicon.

"I'm glad to be back. And that life brought you back here, too. From all that I'm hearing, you're a godsend to the local PD."

She waves my compliment away. "I do my job. I enjoy the challenge of running this team. They're all dedicated pros, right down to the rookie."

"Still defending the officer who puked yesterday, I see." Trinity's loyalty warms my insides, that place inside my ribcage that's been frozen since yesterday.

"Tell me you haven't done the same for one of your sailors."

I remain silent.

She harrumphs in triumph. "So don't go telling me how to handle my officers."

"Mmm. Got it." I wait to throw my next observation out. Sitting in my kitchen has done wonders for my psyche. It's as if the house has its own healing vibe. "Your parents are proud of you, Trinity. You have to know they are." I loved Mr. and Mrs. Colson as much as my own family. They'd put up with Trinity and me and our shenanigans since we'd met in fifth grade.

She sighs. "I do know, but they're not so happy that I'm divorced and raised two kids on my own, for the most part.

It hurt them more than anyone when Raj and I split."

"Breakups are hard all around. Raj has tried to be a good Dad, though, hasn't he?"

"He has." She nods. "He's always been a full co-parent, especially financially. But living in California with his new family and young kids takes away from mine. There's no getting around it."

"You're doing a great job. Look, one already off at college! How are you doing with the empty-nest thing?"

"It's not empty until Elijah leaves next year. He's all wrapped up in his girlfriend, but fortunately between sports and studies there isn't a lot of time left to date. Reggie is doing well in State College, from what he tells me, that is." She grimaced, her eyes rolling. Reggie was a freshman at Penn State's main campus, located in its namesake town of State College, Pennsylvania.

"Boys are so different from girls, I get it. But if it makes you feel any better, the girls haven't been telling me a whole lot of what they're really up to. Their course loads, athletic activities, sure. If they need fast cash, I'm dear sweet Mom again. But on the social scene? Not a peep from either of them. Every time I bring it up, they disconnect."

"Reggie's social scene doesn't worry me. It's the lack of one. He can really isolate, you know?" This was what I missed with Trinity. Sharing the ins and outs of everyday life.

"He's always been brilliant. I know you worry because

you're his Mom, but don't you think he's just miles ahead of his peers?"

"Intellectually, sure. Socially, he's still in grade school." Trinity's phone rings, and she immediately picks it up. "Colson."

I watch her take the call, which appears to be from one of her officers. It's interesting to observe her leadership skills in action. Like me, she's direct and to the point but polite enough about it. Unlike me, she isn't afraid to make her opinion clear.

"I don't want anyone questioning him until I can be there. Got it?"

When Trinity disconnects, she's all business again. "Get your stuff. I need to be at the station."

As I head for my bedroom, hope blooms that maybe Trinity and I will reestablish our friendship after all. There's no reason my hope can't come true, as long as we don't treat one another poorly. It never occurred to me it would be over a murder.

I GRAB A hot chocolate at Latte Love, which is sadly missing Nate behind the counter today, and walk through town. I do my best thinking when I'm in motion. Cold, crisp air tumbles dried leaves, and I remind myself this is my favorite time of year.

Usually, that is. When there's not a murder to solve.

Trinity seemed even more confident when we went back downstairs that I'll be able to get back in my building later today, as several team members reported that they'd wrapped up their portion of the investigation. I took the minimum out of my apartment and dropped it at Skeins and Baahls, where the guys went after breakfast. They want me to come back and "enjoy our trunk show" later but in no way am I ready to carry on with life as usual. Not until I do all I can to put Frannie's memory to rest, and hopefully glean insight into who killed her and why. And why in my building?

It's fair to say it's my responsibility to do what I can to make things right. I know it's not my job to conduct an investigation. Not officially, anyway. But it's my shop, my business, my new life at stake.

I cringe at my lousy metaphor. Will I ever again be able to look at a carved Santa figure as simply a festive decoration? Will anything about Stonebridge, um, Shop 'Round the World, ever not have the pall of Frannie's murder over it?

The answer has to be "yes." Or my new life is over before it's begun.

Chapter Ten

M Y FIRST STOP Sunday afternoon has to be to see Ken. We go back as far as Frannie and I did, and he and I have always shared the same sense of humor and appreciation for the quirkier aspects of Stonebridge. We co-wrote the senior play and received adulation from our classmates and censure from the teachers. In other words, it was a big hit. Especially the skit where we dramatized local celebrities of sorts, and how self-important they behaved. I played the town librarian, who had a particular grudge against high school students using *her* meeting rooms as their personal study halls. Th*at's what a school building's for.* It didn't help that during one of the so-called study sessions Trinity and I organized the best senior prank ever, in my opinion. Ms. Rupp wasn't impressed when the quilters couldn't meet that evening because the room was stuffed with balloons. Well, condoms, that in our defense looked like balloons to the casual observer. Which Ms. Rupp never was, and still isn't. Bless that woman for continuing to run our sturdy library, located in a former grain warehouse built prior to the Civil War. Yes, I said that correctly. Ms. Rupp is now in her mid-seventies and has managed the Stonebridge Library for over forty years.

The memory lifts my heart for a few precious seconds, until I reach the Schrock Real Estate office. Bright multicolored lights flash even in daylight, strewn over the spiral-shaped boxwoods that grow from oversized burnished bronze urns. The turkey and pheasant feather wreath has been replaced by a massive pinecone wreath studded with dried pomegranates. It should encourage me that I'm not the only business in town eager to begin the Christmas season at the risk of skipping Thanksgiving. But no amount of holiday cheer will bring Frannie back or solve her murder. And catch whoever's trying to frame me.

Shock bulldozes me again the moment I step into the lobby. In quintessential Frannie fashion the place is an explosion of tasteful yet pricey holiday decor. Stonebridge is an inclusive, diverse town and the decorations reflect this. A beautiful Victorian Christmas tree stands in the street window alongside a menorah, both surrounded by multicolored lights that are often displayed on Hindu and Sikh homes this time of year. A contemporary nativity carved from local limestone sits on the mantel over the nonfunctioning fireplace in the former residence.

Frannie's assistant Jenna sits at reception, her name boldly printed on a wooden marker. *Jenna Quigley, Executive Assistant.* Is that like assistant to the assistant regional manager?

She's looking down at her phone. When she looks up, her eyes are red-rimmed and puffy. She looks exactly how I feel. Grief stricken.

"Can I help you?" Jenna shows no sign of recognizing me.

"Hi, Jenna. I'm so sorry for your loss. How are you holding up?" I mentally slap myself. Dumb question much?

"This is just awful, Angel." She does recognize me. "We can't believe it." She sniffles. "Why was she in your building to begin with?"

"I… I don't know." Up close, Jenna's grief doesn't take away from the bright intelligence in her eyes. She's a loyal employee from all I've witnessed, and obviously knew how to navigate Frannie's borderline abusive direction like what I overheard on Saturday. It's awful to lose someone you work with day in and day out, no matter how difficult the relationship is. My heart swells for Jenna, having to deal with such a violent reality.

"It doesn't make any sense. Why would someone do that to her? And now we have to worry about a killer being on the loose." More sniffles.

"The police are working it. They'll catch him. Or her." If I say it, it'll happen, right?

"Is it true that you found her? Did you try to save her?" Her watery eyes stare at me but they're vacant again, unseeing. "I mean, was she already—"

I wince. "She was already gone when I got there. There

was nothing I could do."

"I don't understand." She blows her nose, plucks a fresh tissue from a box with Christmas trees printed on it. I vaguely wonder if Frannie picked out the tissue boxes. "She was supposed to meet me and never showed up."

A memory breaks through the fog of emotions coating my thought processes. "After she spoke to you on the phone? She took the call in my office."

She nods, no embarrassment or discomfort at how ill-treated she was by Frannie evident. "Yes. She wanted to meet at Gus's Guitars but never showed. I kept texting her from every place I went over the next few hours..." She doesn't have to say it. Frannie never replied to her texts. It's like reliving the shock of finding Frannie all over again, each time I talk about it. But with my family, I have support and definite suggestions to stay away from the investigation. Jenna's gaze implores me to fix everything, make it all go away.

I'm saved by Ken, who appears from the corridor of offices that run behind Jenna's seat.

"Angel. Come in. Please."

I walk around the reception desk, behind Jenna's seat, and Ken opens his arms. We hug. Ken's grip is almost too tight until his shoulders sag and begin to shake. A harsh sob wrenches from him and brings tears to my eyes.

"Sorry. It's just..." His words are muffled by my coat shoulder, where he's buried his face. I peek at Jenna, and am stopped in my mental tracks by her stare. A split second after our gazes connect her face goes blank again. Does she feel left out of being comforted?

"It's okay, Ken. You need to let it out. Let's go to your office." I keep my arm around him down the hall and up the stairs to the office he shares—shared—with Frannie. Ken remains plastered against my side until we're inside.

Two huge desks face one another across an expanse of pristinely polished birch hardwood. Ken's desk is littered with papers, wadded tissues, a framed photo of Frannie in a striking real estate agent pose in front of what had to be her largest sale, Casting Lodge. The once-derelict property was transformed into a fly fisherman's paradise about ten years ago. No coincidence that it backs up to Jacob's Run, the creek that might have ancient eel weir.

I make a mental note to find out more about the weir and to what Eloise the yoga instructor thinks about them. I wonder if her studio is open on Sundays?

Ken sinks into his chair. "I'm sorry, Angel. I'm not myself."

"You're kidding, right? You just lost your wife, Ken. You're not supposed to be yourself." Tears spring to my eyes for the second time. Not over Frannie but over Ken's loss. I know something, a lot, in fact, about losing a spouse. The one person you counted on to go through all of life, not have them bow out decades sooner than you expected.

I sit on the edge of a leather chair, angled toward Ken.

I'm too keyed up to lean back.

"I don't get it. Why did you need her in your shop to begin with?" His words are a plea for reason, for a way out of his pain. Yet similar enough to Jenna's that I know my worst fears are materializing. People are blaming me for Frannie being in Shop 'Round the World.

My hackles raise in the form of the tiny hairs on my nape bolting straight up. As in, at attention. "I didn't know she was there, Ken. I wasn't in the shop when she...she was killed. She was already gone when I came back from Mass."

At his blank look, I continue. "I need to ask you if you kept a spare copy of the keys. An extra set of keys to my building. I never had the locks changed, so if you did..." My bad, for sure, on the locks. But not a reason for Frannie to enter my building once the sale was final.

"We never keep anyone's keys. They are turned over at closing. Your place is like many of the downtown buildings—you have to have at least a dozen keys on the ring we surrendered."

He was correct. An assortment of keys hung from the large circle, ranging from antique to recently minted at Home Depot. Frannie had made it a point to personally hand the keys over to me in front of Dave, the junior agent who'd done all the work and the mortgage loan officer as we sat at the title company's conference table in downtown Harrisburg.

"Yes, of course." I can't push him, not now. This guy is

definitely at a loss, not the estranged husband Crystal described. Ken's grief feels genuine. Doubt creeps into my awareness nonetheless. Could this all be an act? If it is, Ken's acting ability is super-creepy.

"If you didn't know she was in your shop, then why was she there?" He sighs; a sad, protracted, heart-wrenching sound. Real or not, it triggers the vats of grief I'll never totally be rid of. I grab a tissue.

"I was hoping *you* could tell *me* why she was in there."

Will this get me on the path to finding Frannie's murderer?

Chapter Eleven

W E SIT FOR long minutes, Ken's soft sobs the only breaks in the silence. He leans forward, elbows on his desk, head in hands.

"Frannie might have had one of your keys. She sometimes likes to do follow-up checks on properties. Especially the ones downtown. I've begged her to stop, but she claims it's her right, as she's the only person keeping Stonebridge on the map. It's nothing malicious, Angel. She's looking out for the whole town, truth be told." He's speaking to his closed laptop, his voice low. "We've had complaints from other clients, after the sale is final. About her uninvited entries. You're not the first." His careful choice of words, even in his emotional state, isn't by accident. He's given Frannie's illegal actions a lot of thought, knows she was breaking and entering. Even with a key, she didn't have my, or other building owner's, permission. I keep my observations to myself. For now.

So I wasn't the only one Frannie paid post-closing visits to. And I don't like it that he already knew this about her but tried to shove it on me. Of course, grief can trigger erratic behavior in the best of folks in the best of circumstances. Ken's lost his wife of twenty-plus years to cold-blooded murder.

"I'm not complaining, Ken, really. I'm just wondering why Frannie felt a need to do this." I don't want to upset him further but I have to know. Without all the possible information, how are we going to figure out who killed Frannie, and why?

"Who knows why Frannie does anything she does." Frannie is still alive to him. Not the mental state of a murderer. "She's been obsessed about making Stonebridge the premier tourist destination in Pennsylvania since William was a tot. Her drive to improve the town exploded after he left for the Marines. It's never been enough for her that our business has made more money than we ever imagined. Hell, we have a lifestyle most folks only see on television." Ken speaks like a robot, his words coming out stilted and practiced. He'd had this conversation with Frannie before, no doubt.

"You've worked hard. You both did."

"Frannie wanted people to come here, stay here. Spend all their money downtown. The newer business owners don't want to get wrapped up in all that. They just want to do their work. The long-term owners don't see a need to increase traffic, foot or otherwise, especially during our busy seasons. Which has turned into all year, frankly."

"What specifically did she do to try to get the local business owners on board with her vision?"

"There was no persuasion where Frannie's involved. You knew her, Angel. It's always been her way or the highway. I tried to convince her to stick to total transparency. She'd stop in at a business, check to see if they'd displayed the Stonebridge Business Buddies' pamphlets, especially the one about Stonebridge being Pennsylvania's hidden archaeological gem. The eel weir hasn't been authenticated, but she didn't want to wait and Frannie produced it herself, without getting the Buddies' approval."

"You can't fault her for being driven. Or her unwavering belief in Stonebridge." No matter her motives. If Frannie were a man, less attention, if any, would be given to her more aggressive tactics. Save for the breaking and entry.

"It was illegal according to the letter of the law, and even if everyone around here knows each other, treats one another like family, it was unprofessional. Frannie angered many. Oh, why, why couldn't she let it go? She'd still be alive." His head hangs low between broad shoulders.

I stand up and grab a box of tissues—with the same pattern as the ones in the lobby—walk around his desk. I place a hand on his shoulder. Words won't help, not now. If they did, it wouldn't matter because I can't come up with anything.

I'm mulling over the fact that Frannie may have been in the wrong place at the wrong time, all because she wanted to see if I'd set up a local information display. I hadn't, not yet.

She'd only left the brochures that morning.

Not that I ever intended to use precious merchandising space for paper handouts. The Stonebridge Historical Society has its own building, a three-hundred-year-old cabin located two blocks up from the main drag. There's a quaint information booth in the adjacent parking lot. I'm happy to direct customers there, as I'd assume are the other shop owners. Retail area in our historical buildings is at a minimum and every inch counts.

Before worries about my shop take root in my brain I try to think of what I can do for Ken.

"Have you told William?"

He blows his nose, nods. "The Red Cross is sending a message. I couldn't reach him. He's out in the field." That answers it. Ken doesn't need my help as he's already figured out the quickest way to reach his US Marine Corps son.

"They'll get a hold of him in no time. It's what they do."

"That's what they tell me." He shakes his head. "I hate to drag him into this."

"His mother's death?" How on earth did he think it was *dragging* his son into it, unless—

"No, no, not that, of course not. Yes, I don't want to have to let him know his mother's gone, and especially how she died. But now everything will come out. It always does when people die."

My mental warning bells are chiming and the tune isn't *Ode to Joy.*

"What so you mean by *everything*?" I ignore my guilt over asking such a personal question when I think I may already know the answer. My respect for Trinity's vocation increases. I thought I had the corner on professional focus, but trying to investigate a murder is beyond challenging. How does she do this, day in and day out? I'd ask her but that would mean letting her know what I'm up to, and let's just say that until I can take something solid to her, it's not worth risking she'll tell me to cease and desist.

"Come on, Angel. You've been back home long enough. I'm sure you've heard all about the troubles Frannie and I have had over the years. For all I know, the guy she had the one-nighter with has something to do with this."

Whoa. He's confirming Frannie's affair?

"I'd heard you two ran into a rough patch a few years ago. But, ah, I thought you two worked things out?"

"'Rough patch.' That's a polite way of saying our marriage is over. When the crap hit the fan the first time, several years ago, it was my fault. I strayed. But yeah, we got past it. We decided that we had too much shared history together to throw it down the drain. I thought we were doing so much better. We were. I'm certain of it. That's why it was so hard when someone I trusted told me about her recent affair. When I confronted her about it, she didn't deny it, but wouldn't tell me who it was with. Believe me, in the moment when I found out that she'd stepped out of our marriage, after all that effort, all the counseling, the fancy *dates*,—he makes air quotes—"I would have welcomed her departure from my life."

I sit straight up, wondering if it's this easy. Is Ken the murderer?

"Oh my God." His eyes widen, lock on mine. "I don't mean I'd have killed her, though. God, no!" More tears well, making his eyes a brilliant shade of aquamarine. "You know what I mean, you must have been upset with your husband from time to time." He stops himself short, stands up. Gets us each a water bottle from a mini-fridge.

"I'm sorry, Angel. You don't need to hear all of this. I'm sorry Frannie picked your shop to do her snooping in."

"Me, too." I'm willing to let Ken's careless comment about Tom go. Ken's in an ugly place. But my forgiveness doesn't lessen the sting of his words, the reminder that I don't have Tom's arms to comfort me and take away the stress of the last twenty-four hours. Unlike Ken and Frannie, Tom and I had a solid relationship. A loving one. A pang for my claw-foot tub and gallons of hot water strikes. A steaming soak isn't the same as Tom, but it has its own therapeutic qualities.

"I'll leave you be for now, Ken. Let me kn—"

"Ken, man, I'm so sorry." The greeting cuts through my farewell. A burly man about our age stands at the door, his face creased with concern. Ken looks over, waves him in.

I nod at the stranger, then give Ken a quick hug. "Call me if there's anything you need, no matter how small."

But he's already talking to the man I've never met. I let myself out, taking the back stairs and exiting onto the side alley. Before I'm back on Main Street, I'm wondering who I should speak with next. And more pressing, I need to find out if it's true Frannie was in the midst of an extracurricular sexual relationship, as recently as now, and with whom.

What about why?

Nope. Frannie's motives for cheating on Ken aren't my business.

Maybe I need to tell Trinity I'm doing some of my own investigating, after all. She'd tell me to let the pros handle it, and I get it, I do. And unless I find out something I think she can use, there's no sense bothering her. Plus I'm still sensing that while my alibis cleared me of suspicion, I'm not in a position to push my luck with SPD. Not until I know that Trinity completely trusts me.

Finding out some details that could help solve the murder is a great place to start. It's not like there's any risk to me.

Chapter Twelve

M Y LIST OF suspects is long, too long, considering that Frannie seems to have ticked off most of Stonebridge's small business community. Navy training comes to my rescue again as I recall how I memorized the litany of flight rules for a helicopter.

Knock off the bigger suspects off first.

Er, maybe *knock off* isn't the right term here. I've already visited Ken, and I'll have to circle back to him after his initial period of shock passes. When it won't feel so much like I'm being an opportunist.

Since she came up in two separate conversations with two different people, Eloise is my next target. Lucky for me a quick search on my phone reveals her yoga studio is open today. Even better, a class is about to let out. The studio is only two blocks away, so I burrow into my coat and lean against a sycamore tree while I answer some texts. I'd like to meet with Frannie alone, sans her yoginis.

My stomach plummets when I see all the missed texts from Ava and Lily. They tried to call my for our weekly Sunday video chat. Since I'd put my phone on *do not disturb* while I was with Ken, I'd missed them. Two hours ago, their gentle reminders were typical.

From Ava: "*Mom, we know you're busy setting up the first glimpse of global living that Stonebridge has ever seen, but we're your daughters. Call us.*"

And from Lily: "*Speak for yourself, Ava. I understand that you're under the gun, Mom. If you can't talk now, we can call later tonight.*"

But only fifteen minutes ago, both girls were clearly uncomfortable.

From Lily: *"MOM ARE YOU OUT THERE? SEND PROOF OF LIFE (a photo of Ralph works)"*

And then, Ava: "*Mom, don't worry, we're not freaking out but we would like to know you're okay.*"

As I stare at my screen, it indicates an incoming video call from Ava. Eldest by seven minutes is eldest no matter what.

I connect. A few seconds later Lily connects, and all three of us are grinning at each other.

"Mom, where are you?"

"Me? Oh, I'm standing outside. It's a beautiful day here." Cold rain hits my cheeks and I smear a drop off the screen.

"You're going to get the cold front we had here last night. Lily you're next, so no more crop tops."

Lily sticks out her tongue, making Ava roll her eyes before they both explode into peals of giggles. An entire state between them, with Ava in Pittsburgh and Lily in Philadelphia, and their bond is only stronger.

Their constant joking and twin telepathy can be downright annoying, but today it sounds like the most beautiful symphony. I blink back tears, wipe my eye.

"Mom? What's going on?"

"Nothing. It's the wind, it's picked up a bit." I don't have to fake the shiver that rattles my shoulders.

"Why don't you like, I don't know, go inside?" Lily is a very helpful eighteen-year-old.

"You're not her mother, baby sis." Ava peers at me. "But Lily is right. Maybe you should take the call inside. Do you want to call us back in a few?"

"Ye—um, er, no, I can't. Lots going on." I'm relieved that Frannie's death hasn't hit the news outlets yet. Not that it matters. Local news, Stonebridge news, isn't something the girls follow. If it doesn't come through their social media feeds or scrolls, it didn't happen in their world. But I don't want them shocked when they find out, which they will. They like to call Bryce, and he has a hard time keeping anything a secret when it comes to his nieces.

I listen as each daughter fills me in on her studies, extracurriculars. I get that they're not telling me everything they do, but do I really need to know? Do I *want* to know? I'm relieved to hear their voices, to know they're both doing so well.

Their Mom, not so much.

"Look, girls, I don't want to worry you but I've had an

incident in the shop." Before either of them can interrupt me, I fill them in, leaving out grisly details.

"OMG Mom!"

"Whoo hoo, Mom's a badass!"

Well. That went better than I'd hoped.

"When can you go back home?"

"By the end of today. Look, I need to go. I love you both and can't wait for Thanksgiving. We're going to have the best time ever."

"Can you leave the tape outline of the body for us to look at?" Lily, already declared a Criminal Forensics major, has been taking notes the entire time, I'm certain.

"Doubtful, dumb a—"

"Ava!"

We finish up with promises that I'll keep them informed, and they won't talk about it at school. It's an ongoing investigation, after all.

I disconnect and note that it's exactly fifteen minutes since I stopped to gather my thoughts. And the perfect time to catch Eloise alone, with an hour between her Sunday yoga classes.

"BRING IT IN, girlfriend!" Eloise opens her arms wide and all at once I'm engulfed in her namaste embrace and a cloud of patchouli. It's like hugging serenity. I hug back, thanking the yoga goddesses that my plan worked and Eloise is indeed alone. "You must be a wreck! I heard what happened."

"What have you heard, exactly?"

"That Frannie was found murdered in your shop."

Wow. So much for keeping anything quiet for more than a nanosecond in this town.

"Yeah, that about sums it up."

"But you're not a suspect, or you'd be locked up, right?"

"Uh, no, I don't believe I'm a suspect at this point. I wasn't there when it happened."

Eloise shakes her head. "It's a damn shame, a shock. But…"

"But?"

"Never mind. You've caught me at a good time. I'm in between classes." Eloise is the picture of yoga exuberance with her lotus-imprinted headband, long single braid, and coordinated tank top, sweater, and tights. Her toes are painted in the same hue of violet as her clothing.

"Oh, well, I don't want to take up your break."

"You're not! Come on back and I'll make you a green tea. You drink tea? Or I have water if you'd prefer." We cross the spacious studio to a nook defined by an ornate room divider. Teak, if my eye is correct.

"Tea's fine. Thank you." I'm going to be swimming in coffee and tea by the end of the day, but if I get some answers it's worth it. Does Trinity need to drink a lot of coffee or tea, too, to stay alert through her investigations?

Eloise carefully measures leaves into a handless mug and pours hot water from a water cooler unit over them, a very Pennsylvanian take on the ritual.

"Have a seat." She nods at a beanbag chair, and I shrug out of my coat, sink into the kind of seat I haven't used since I was in middle school. I hope I can get out of it gracefully when I need to. "Here."

The mug is warm but not too hot, and the tea, delicious. Eloise sits in a low-slung canvas folding chair kitty-corner from me.

"What a beautiful space, Eloise!" No effort is needed to compliment the large, high-ceilinged room. "How did you get the sky lights in there?"

"You mean after we removed the entire second floor? It was a process, let me tell you. We had to put the loft in afterward, as a whole new structure. I was so excited to be able to buy this, right here on Main Street, that I underestimated the renovation costs."

"I'm going through my own renovations, but nothing this extensive." I watch her, try to do what I think a detective would. Observe. Her perfectly messy bun shows off her golden highlights, which in turn accent her sable eyes. Eyes that laughed with me through plenty of Stonebridge High School cross-country meets. "Who'd have thought that when we were running through the hills around town we'd ever own businesses on Main Street?"

Her eyes widen. "It's no coincidence, if you ask me."

"Oh?"

"There's a special kind of energy here. Our town rests atop the remains of an ancient civilization, after all." She holds her arms out to her side, palms out, as if she's a human whirligig. "The chakra pulses aren't old, or new, but eternal."

"Do you mean Native American?"

"Of course. You've heard about the brouhaha over the eel weir in Jacob's Run, haven't you?"

It's why I'm here. And why I'm wondering why she doesn't seem to want to talk about Frannie anymore. "Yes but I'm under the impression that the grad students from Penn State haven't determined if it's truly prehistoric, or built by the colonists, or more recent."

Eloise's brow disappears under her headband. "Tell me you don't feel it, Angel?"

Oh no. She's mistaken interest for some kind of chakra enlightenment. It'd be flat-out rude to stop her narration, though. She's throwing herself into it full throttle.

"The weirs, *our* weir, predates the pyramids, Angel. I know you sense the energy they're still sending us." She waves her hands around her body, as if spirits of the past will materialize at any moment.

I consider myself an open-minded person. Especially for someone who's spent half of her life following very definite rules, regulations, and procedures. Do I believe in what Eloise is describing? Energy fields, for example?

Well, I don't disbelieve, let me put it that way. No sailor

or pilot is being honest if they don't admit to at least a little bit of believing in something greater than themselves. We're a notoriously superstitious lot. But it's not something I really want to spend time discussing when I'm under the gun to solve a murder or face business failure.

"I heard that Frannie was excited about the weir. She thought it would triple our tourism."

Eloise's mouth twists into a sneer. No hint of serenity. "Frannie was an opportunist. That's okay, it was always her calling to be a businessperson. But there has to be a line when profit motives overreach."

My heart stops then kick starts into overdrive. Was Frannie admitting something here? As in, murder?

"I take it you and Frannie didn't agree."

"Don't play coy, Angel. We've known one another a long time, and it's clear to me we're both following our hearts with what we're establishing on Main Street. Trust me, you would have been fighting Frannie's strong-arm tactics along with the rest of us. If she'd lived." Eloise shakes her head. "I said I wasn't surprised by her death, the murder, because she's stirred up so much trouble over turning Stonebridge into Frannietown. The weir was but one symptom of her obsession. I am sorry, of course, that she suffered, that it came to this."

"So you believe someone in town killed her? A business owner?"

She blinks as if registering what I'm saying. "Honestly? I

highly doubt anyone here would have wished her dead. But if she was that forceful with folks she knew, people she'd made a lot of money from over the years, how brutal must she have been with outsiders?"

"Outsiders?"

"Investors from out of state, out of country. Schrock Real Estate handled both residential and commercial properties, and Frannie was always in the business of enticing investors for her pet projects like the Stoppe and Shoppe."

"That's a lot to consider, Eloise. I appreciate your frankness. I'm a bit at a loss, being new. Sure, I grew up here, but I've been out of the Stonebridge loop."

Eloise stands up, and I try to. Except the beanbag has my bottom feeling like it weighs a ton. I hand Eloise my teacup and roll onto all fours, then stand.

"I guess I could use some yoga practice."

Eloise has the grace to smile without judgment. "My next class is due in soon, but we should plan time together." She places the mugs in the tiny sink then walks to another counter and reaches for a large phone. Its protective case sports yet another lotus flower. "Let's share numbers."

"Uh, okay, sure." I reach down for my purse, grab my phone. We exchange contact information in silence.

As she walks me to the exit, Eloise hands me a business card that's a coupon for a free class. "Next week, the Tuesday-Thursday ten o'clock is for yoga newbies." She gives me another quick hug before I slip out the door. The cold

November wind slaps my cheeks and any warm and fuzzy comfort Eloise and her yoga studio offered is scrubbed clean. I'd be happy to reconnect, especially if it turns out Eloise didn't murder Frannie. I don't get a sense that she did, or is capable of it, but what do I know?

Not a lot, except that Frannie's possible murderer list remains overwhelming. I look over my shoulder as I start walking toward Skeins and Baahls and catch Eloise standing at the large picture window of her studio, the artistically lettered ELOISE'S ENERGY YOGA arced over her head, GIVE US A WHORL stenciled at her feet. When our gazes connect, it's with none of the warmth of her welcome.

I'll hold off on the yoga for a bit.

FIFTEEN MINUTES LATER I'm at the other end of town, a couple blocks off Main Street. I'm grateful that the guys convinced me—okay, pleaded via multiple texts since breakfast—to stop in for their trunk show. I know they're worried about me, and instead of annoying me as Bryce often can, it feels good to be close to family for this very reason.

Skeins and Baahls is a respite from the busy street outside, symbolic of how knitting gives me a break from the constant hamster wheel otherwise known as my mind. It's funny how I could always focus on a Navy mission but take

me out of the cockpit or now, out of my shop, and I floun-
der. Having needles and yarn in my hands helps. But my
hands are so dry and nicked with paper cuts from the
constant unpacking of merchandise that the mere thought of
doing something with them makes my raw skin hurt. And
truth be told I can't allow myself to numb out with anything
right now. Not while a murderer lurks in my town.

Bryce arranges their stock by color instead of weight, so
no matter what you want to knit, you simply find the hue
you want and match it to the fiber you need. The wall of
rainbow-ordered skeins lifts my spirits every time I walk in.

I meander around the shop while Bryce and Nico attend
to customers. When they leave I stop pacing, take my coat
off, and sit down at the communal crafting area.

"This is the perfect yarn for you, sister." Bryce holds up
two balls of bulky, as in really thick, yarn. One skein is navy
blue and the other, gold. We're in the coziest part of the yarn
shop, and I'm sitting on the bright lime green loveseat while
Bryce shows off the mound of fine fibers displayed on a live-
edge coffee table. Nico's in the far corner, brewing up
espresso for all three of us. "Or try the new Angora-cashmere
blend. Here, this is your color." He holds a rosy pink up to
my cheeks. "And we have a new selection of ergonomic
needles you have to try. On us."

"Mmm." I don't want to admit that Ralph gnawed another pair of bamboo knitting needles. I keep meaning to
switch to metal needles but I like the comfort of wood if I'm

going to take the time to sit and stitch. A rare event these past several weeks, and now, forget it. "I don't need more yarn, not until I get into a regular routine, after the shop opens. Besides, what would I make for myself with that?"

"You're back in North America, honey. Pennsylvania, no less. The winters are *brrrrr* cold!" Bryce's trying too hard but I know his motive. He's always considered it his job to make me laugh when I'm bummed. I wish it could be over an unrequited middle-school crush instead of a murder.

"It's no colder here than Belgium was. You get more snow, sure."

"Pulllleeeze. Does *polar vortex* mean anything to you?" As Bryce pontificates, Nico hands me a tiny white porcelain cup with matching saucer, as there's no room on the table.

"Polar what?"

"It's the weather pattern that brought below zero temps last year."

"You mean wind chills, right?" The espresso is hot and has the bite I need. "Nico, this is so good. Just what I need to fuel my work tonight."

"You can't be serious. You are not going to work alone in that shop while there's a murderer on the loose!" Bryce claws at his throat and takes a seat into the faux-fur easy chair. "I still can't believe you're willing to stay in your building at all, frankly."

"Trinity's cleared it. My biggest threat upstairs is Mom breaking in unannounced. The police are watching the building 24/7, and I'm having a full-blown security system installed tomorrow." It's going to cost thousands more than I originally budgeted for a security system, which was zero. Sure, I'd planned put in one of those basic systems with a few cameras, one on each door and one for the retail space. Someday. It wasn't a priority when I thought I was moving back to the Stonebridge I grew up in.

"Well, whoever killed Frannie, God rest her soul, wanted to implicate you. Don't forget that."

"Why do you think I'm doing some of my own investigating? I'm very aware that I'm not a professional investigator or detective, but the sooner SPD solves this, the better." I finish the coffee. Bryce and Nico exchange exasperated looks.

"Stop it, you two. I'm a grown woman. I'm smart enough to not step on Trinity's toes with my snooping." And I'm going to tell Trinity all that I find out. Which isn't a whole lot so far.

"Angel darling, have you given any further thought to attending the Stonebridge Small Business Buddies meeting Tuesday night? It's the quickest way to get you plugged into the community. You know, to cement the roots you're putting down." Nico sits beside me, resting his arm along the back of the loveseat.

I try to not physically squirm as my internal alarm bells, already jangled by finding Frannie, rally to yet another crescendo. What I haven't mentioned to my family, to anyone, is that joining anything local feels constricting. If Shop 'Round the World doesn't work out, if Stonebridge doesn't work out for me, it'll be easier to pick up and find another place to start over. No, I've no intention of moving again. Yes, I know this is a major holdover from moving every two years for the last quarter of a century. No, this isn't the time to psychoanalyze myself.

Both men's gazes are steady on me.

"I was going to wait until the shop opened. I'm so far behind my schedule after losing last night and all day today." Although, now that I needed to figure out who the last people were to see Frannie alive, it might not be a bad idea to go.

Nico takes my cup and walks it to the small counter on the wall behind the cash register. "It starts at seven P.M., on the dot. Of course being on time isn't a problem for you."

Nico's assumption is a common one. That my military background means I'm a stickler for details and promptness. In truth, I suppose I am.

So why haven't I unearthed any details on Frannie's killer yet?

BACK IN MY home after getting the okay from Trinity, I go to bed early, hoping that sleep will release me from the awfulness of Frannie's murder. Lying under my down comforter, I listen to Ralph's gentle breathing. I rolled his cage into my bedroom, my only acquiescence to feeling a bit unnerved. Plus my phone resting next to my pillow, with Trinity, SPD, and Cumberland County Emergency Services all on speed dial.

I'm exhausted and not surprised that I start to drift off within minutes. But not before I imagine the intense anger it had to have taken to shove Frannie against the storage shelving hard enough to kill her.

If I can figure out who was angry enough to do that, I'll find her murderer.

Chapter Thirteen

"THAT LOOKS GOOD, Max." Late Monday morning I try to muster enthusiasm as I speak to Phil's carpenter. He's called me out of my office to show me the floating shelves, hung and stained. It's quiet and still and I'm finding it hard to break the silence except when I have to. It's almost as if the building knows it's where a soul left the planet.

"I'm sorry to interrupt your work but I didn't want to leave until I knew you're happy."

Max's eyelids droop as he gives Ralph, perched on my shoulder, a side-eye but he says nothing about my green buddy. Ralph has been especially needy since Saturday and it's easier for me to keep him with me than have him scream his new mystery word from his perch. Allowing Ralph to sleep in my bedroom hasn't kept him from clinging to me all morning. He's so codependent. I adjust his too-sharp claws as I deal with Max.

"It's exactly what I wanted. Your attention to detail is off the charts. Thank you."

"I had to cut the longest one short by a few inches, to fit snug in the corner." He points to the retail area's back southern wall, which it shares with the storage room. Where Frannie was…

I shut down the mental trip to Feartown as best I can. No amount of pilot training on compartmentalization is going to erase the knowledge of Frannie's suffering, but I have to try. For my sake, my family's, the town's.

For all of us.

"That's fine, Max. It all looks better than I imagined." My fingers itch to start putting up the merchandise displays. A tiny, familiar spark ignites deep in my chest. Enthusiasm for the shop, for my future in Stonebridge.

"*Eeeeeetch!*" Ralph screams in my ear and his claw tips dig into my hand-knit sweater. So much for soothing him.

"Stop that, Ralph." I reach up and scratch his nape, which calms him. "You're a good boy." It's always there between Ralph and me, this constant thrum that I imagine is our connection. Now I feel he's trying to tell me "I know who killed Frannie." But does he? Did he really see anything, or just hear the murder? I shudder at the thought of what her last moments sounded like.

"Do you want me to change anything?" Max's concern reflects more emotion the man's emitted since I met him. Normally a *hey, bro'* type of dude, I realize he's been grim since arriving back to work earlier. And more pointedly, he hasn't ventured anywhere near the back office, storage room, or entrance, opting to bring all his supplies through the front customer door. The woodworking tools were moved out here by the forensics team and Max didn't so much as ask to move them back into my office.

"No, not at all. You've done a great job, Max. And listen. I know it's hard, being here right now. Working in a place where someone died. I. Know I'm distracted, and it's my shop."

"The place where Frannie was murdered, you mean." He nods stoically. "I know she had to save her marriage, but it doesn't take away from what we shared, you know?" His eyes cast downward, as if searching the sawdust for a tiny insect. "It's hard." A huge tear trembles at the edge of his lower lid, then decides to take the leap and rolls down his chiseled cheek.

I have to give Stonebridge men credit for feeling their feelings, and not being afraid to show them. But why in front of me?

"I didn't realize you knew Frannie." Before I finish my observation, it hits me. Max could be Frannie's lover.

Holy cannoli!

Easy, easy. Take it slow.

"Um, so you two were, close friends?"

"More than that. The whole town knows, Ms. Angel." His eyes finally meet mine. "You're shocked, it seems, but Frannie's not the first mature woman I've been with. People say I have an old soul, so older women are a natural fit for me. I'm twenty-eight and I've never dated a woman under thirty-five, even ten years ago." He looks at me meaningfully.

"You know, attraction doesn't see the years." He raises a brow.

How I keep from laughing or gasping is beyond me, but somehow I'm able to dig deep for a neutral demeanor. "I'm sorry for your loss, Max. I didn't realize you and Frannie were currently involved."

"Oh, we weren't. I mean we were, all last week. But then, well, we had to break it off. She told me on Saturday." If he realizes he just admitted to a motive to kill Frannie, he doesn't show it.

"This past Saturday? That's awful. I mean, that your last interaction wasn't a positive one. Can I ask what time you last saw Frannie?" Prying when a potential suspect is at their emotional bottom is becoming too easy for my conscience, even with pragmatic reasons for doing so.

Max looks at the floor, scratches his neck. Doesn't make eye contact. "It was sometime after I ran into you that morning. I knew it was coming, you know? I just didn't want to see the signs. But we were through at least a week ago."

"Signs?"

"She kept talking about going on vacation with Ken. To a romantic spot. Not something you do when you're going to choose your boyfriend over your husband."

"No, I suppose it's not." He seems truly sad, just like Ken did. But wouldn't a murderer be cold-blooded enough to be able to put on a show?

Ralph starts to preen my hair, making soft cooing noises. Max finally looks up at both of us.

"If you don't mind, Ms. Angel, I need the rest of the day off. I've got to process this, man."

"You work for Phil, not me. But I'm okay with you knocking off until tomorrow. All that's left is the cashier's counter." I almost say *plan on taking time off for the funeral, too* but the date to lay Frannie to rest hasn't been set. Since her body had to go to Lehigh Valley for the autopsy, it could be another few days or so.

"Thanks. I'll see you tomorrow, then." He gathers his personal tools, and departs through the front door, his shoulders slung low. I briefly watch as he slings the large canvas duffle into the bed of his pickup. Neither Ken nor Max can come off my suspect list. Not by a long shot.

I lock the door and turn back to my office. I've avoided the storeroom and can't blame Max for steering clear of the back of the shop. The police are done with their investigation and the cleaning crew I hired came in when I opened this morning and took care of scrubbing the shelf and floor. If I didn't know Frannie's body had been there, I wouldn't be able to tell anything awful had happened.

But I do know. The memory's like a brand that's still smoking on my brain.

Still, it's important to move on, keep going with my plans. Life is for the living and all that. But it's also true that justice matters.

Before I can convince myself to stay in the too-quiet building, I make a decision.

"Come on, Ralph. Let's get you upstairs."

"YOU'RE KIDDING! HE confessed to the affair then and there?" Crystal's eyes bug out behind her glasses, her arms elbow-deep in the cut flowers she's arranging for a customer, working through her usual noon lunchtime. A lot of red and white carnations, interspersed with noble fir branches. A large red vase waits on the stainless work counter for the festive bouquet.

I couldn't bear to talk to her on the phone, or wait until she gets off work. I rationalize the thirty-minute roundtrip drive is part of my necessary workday. After all, I won't be fruitful with my own business until I have solid answers.

"He did." I notice that all of her bouquets appear to be Christmas themed. "Where are your Thanksgiving arrangements?"

She wipes her forehead with the back of her hand. "In the storage refrigerator. I've delivered the vast majority of them. We're getting close and my customers seem to want the Christmas decor earlier each year."

"Speaking of which, any chance you can make room for a large Christmas centerpiece for the shop?" I was already counting on the Thanksgiving arrangement she'd promised for our family turkey dinner.

"I already did. Remind me to show you."

Comfort in the form of fuzzy warmth around my center makes me smile. "You're the best big sister ever."

We're at Crystal's workbench, behind the small storefront of the nursery she runs. It's adjacent to Brad's landscaping business which is basically a converted antique barn that houses all of his equipment. A graveled road winds around to the back of it, where pile upon pile of everything from river rocks to mushroom compost reside. Crystal's flower fields occupy a few acres on the other side of the supply storage. As I drove in, I caught glimpses of the battered gray sunflower fields, their cheery autumnal hues snuffed out by our first frost last month.

Crystal and Brad established Finnegan's Lawn & Landscaping almost thirty years ago. The florist part is all Crystal's baby, with cut flowers her specialty. Crystal owns the floral and nursery part of the company outright since she decided she needed to be "more than a wife and mother 24/7." The annual contracts she receives from several south central Pennsylvania catering firms are enough to entirely cover her overhead. She handles several business offices, too, ensuring their lobbies are never without the most current seasonal decor.

"Hmmm. So Max and Frannie. You say he's not more than thirty? Wow. That puts a new spin on the whole story, doesn't it? Do you think he did it?" Crystal never stops working as she helps me sift through the facts.

"He's twenty-eight, for the record. I have no idea who did it, but he has a dang good motive, wouldn't you say? Also, for the record, you didn't mention this at Latte Love on Saturday." I hand her the noble fir stem she's reaching for. "Does that make sense to you, though? That Frannie was stepping out on Ken so recently? With this guy Max? You'd said that they'd made up, moved on from their transgressions. Well, his, anyway. I thought all that was behind them."

"Hmm. What Max said about the entire town knowing—it's a bit of an exaggeration. I didn't mention it because while I've heard a rumor or two about her in the last weeks, I didn't think it was anything more than malicious gossip, most likely from one of the small business owners she was haranguing to get in step with the Frannie Stonebridge agenda. You know she wasn't one to make bosom buddies with anyone, not where hardcore business was involved. Some folks tried to say her beau was underage, but the kibosh was put on that by Ken, actually. He confided in Brad that he'd forgiven her for what he thought her one-time fling, and told him the guy was in his twenties." Brad and Ken were fishing buddies.

"When they had their troubles two years ago, are you certain Frannie wasn't cheating then, too?" Not that I want more suspects on my list, but I'd hate to overlook anyone obvious.

Crystal pushes her glasses up from where they've slipped to the tip of her nose. "There were rumors back then that Frannie's flirting with other men was a bit over the top, but nothing substantial. Ken's definitely the one who had the affair back then."

"I know about that, then." I don't want to betray Ken's confidence even to Crystal. No matter that he's still on my suspect list, it's too skeevy to break trust given during such extreme sorrow.

"You're not a gossiping type, Angel. Since when have you become the gatherer of all things Stonebridge?"

"Since I found Frannie dead in my shop. Murdered. Like, only two days ago." I'm trying to keep our banter in the sisterly zone we both love, but I can't keep the strain out of my tone. I'm looking pretty worn out, too. When I woke up this morning, I had what seemed a brilliant idea to honor Frannie. I was going for a low-key holiday theme when I dressed in my favorite red ski sweater, green corduroy short skirt, and matching green tights with glitter snowflakes. But I've caught a glimpse or two of myself through the day and my hair's out of control, highlighting the serious bags under my eyes. Add in the coating of sawdust over my outfit and I'm passing more as the town's bedraggled elf.

"Sorry, sis. You've been through the wringer. And you're not out of it yet."

"Tell me about it. I'm not upset with you, Crystal."

"I know that, Angel. Yeah, Ken's affair was in full Technicolor, surround sound and all. At one point he shacked up with her in her apartment. Oh, sorry. You need to know who. It was Liza, the assistant at the real estate office."

"She must have been there before Jenna, then. Jenna's the only assistant I know of."

Crystal nods. "Yes, the one assistant stayed on, but Liza left. They looked for a replacement quickly but I don't think they ever found one. Frannie even went so far as to ask me if I had a few hours a week to spare. It was hard times finding hourly employees that year, and then there's Frannie's reputation as a less-than-ideal boss. Her former reputation, that is." Crystal sighs. "It's so sad, really. I don't think either of them, Ken or Frannie, ever have been truly happy."

"I'm surprised you didn't say more yesterday at the coffee shop."

"We got a little sidetracked after you caught a glimpse of Nate the barista, remember?"

Nate. Yeah, I remembered. "Feels more like two months ago than just Saturday." When I'd allowed myself that little thrill of attraction.

Crystal's gaze turns critical, and she sets her flower trimmers on the tattered workbench. "You need a break. Why don't you go to the house and catch a catnap? There are no reminders of murder in our guest room."

I wave away her concern. "I got a good night's in my own bed last night. Besides the shock of it all, I can't say I feel that stressed." Except for the possibility of the shop not opening on time part.

"Uh huh. Because you get interrogated by Stonebridge's lead detective every day."

"Trinity's cleared me as a suspect. My alibis all checked out and I have zero motive. As we both know."

Crystal sets the vase aside, picks out several different types of bare branches from her buckets, and begins arranging them in a barrel-shaped vase. "The problem is that too many people in Stonebridge have motive. The question is, who had the wherewithal to take it to such a grisly end?"

Chapter Fourteen

CRYSTAL'S QUESTION HAUNTS me when I get back into town. Too wound up to enclose myself in the office, I promise Ralph I'll be back in a few and head out for a run.

Okay, a fast walk. Running has never been my go-to exercise. Give me a road bike and miles of rural highway any day. But for now, a walk is the quickest way I'll tire myself out enough to contemplate a long soak in the tub, followed by hopefully a solid slumber. I lied to Crystal about sleeping well last night.

Main Street is congested as the earliest commuters pass through on their way home from Harrisburg or further. Every single parking spot is occupied, and people wrapped in warm outerwear thread down the sidewalks, going in and out of the shops. The thrill that gave me butterflies over this business potential isn't there, and I make a quick left to enter an alley that will take me to the road that leads out of town. It's still light out, but I'm not willing to run on the shoulder no matter how much reflective gear I wear, so as soon as I reach the entrance to a subdivision I angle in, mindful of turning cars.

Cumberland Cove is the quintessential mid-century neighborhood, with mature oak and mulberry trees on either side of the wide streets. Low-slung split-levels sit far enough back from the road to see them, but allow for ample privacy. Many houses are in the processes of being decked out for the holidays and I focus on each home in an effort to clear my mind. A large air-filled turkey gently waves in the breeze on one lawn, while a set of Charlie Brown characters from the Christmas special hang out on another. Most houses already have lights strung, a smart tactic when the weather can change on a dime this time of year. Plus, several Stonebridge families celebrate Diwali by hanging multicolored lights, which adds to the sense of being in the middle of celebration.

The tension in my shoulders eases and I can almost pretend that Saturday didn't happen. Almost, for just this tiny sliver of time.

I walk past the house I considered buying before I realized I'd be much happier living atop the shop. Plus the numbers crunched out better.

The twins had preferred the stone-front house, especially the kidney-shaped pool complete with waterfall nestled in the backyard. The FOR SALE sign is gone, so I assume it sold. I haven't thought to check in the flurry of the past few months. I won—

"Woof!"

A Sasquatch-sized canine leaps in front of me a split second after his warning bark. I freeze, hold up my arms. I know I shouldn't make eye contact but this looks more like a wolf, with amber eyes to match.

My adrenaline spikes my heart rate as, you guessed it, good ol' Navy training kicks in. *Stay calm. No sudden moves. Be the alpha!* The last is Crystal's admonition every time I encounter her three burly labs, whom I adore.

"It's okay, boy? Good doggie." I use my lowest voice and pray the dog doesn't notice my knocking knees.

But this is a strange dog and I'm a stranger in what I assume is his neighborhood. He's stopped barking and moves in close, sniffing me. He's the biggest German shepherd I've ever met, and some detached part of me wonders if I shouldn't be peeing my workout pants about now.

"Mach!" A loud booming voice, this one human, thank the feral pets goddess, makes the dog's ears pointier than possible and his head whips to the source. Who names their dog after Mach speed? Although I have to admit it fits. This wolf came out of nowhere.

A tall, slim man strides toward us across the front lawn of the house I considered buying, his brows drawn together in disapproval. My defenses lock in and I'm ready to fire.

"You need to keep your dog on a leash."

"Mach, stay." The man's still several yards out, but close enough that I make out his face. And the silver hair that tops it. The butterflies in my stomach activate.

"Nate the barista." Did I say it aloud?

He halts, as quickly as Mach did on his master's command. "Yes. Oh, hi again." Nate barely glances at me. "Come here, boy." He slaps his thigh and Mach trots to his master. With zero fuss he allows Nate to snap an Eagles leash on the Phillies collar I hadn't noticed.

Nate straightens, his gaze laser-focused on me. Butterfly activity increases.

"I'm sorry about that. I hope Mach didn't frighten you too badly."

"Oh, no, he's a sweetheart of a boy." Oops. Sarcasm is my go-to when I'm discombobulated. "It's…it's fine."

"No, it's not, is it, Mach?" He shoots the dog a stern glance and I realize his annoyance is with Mach, not me. I let out a breath.

"That's a cool name for a dog. Are you a pilot?"

Puzzled lines appear between very nice brows that top even nicer eyes. Yep, still sexy gray. "Ah, no." Realization dawns in the form of a quick laugh, which makes sexy Nate more appealing. Friendly. As if we could become friends. "His name isn't Mach like Mach 1. You mean the speed of sound, right?"

I nod, embarrassed. I have a way of making everything about me when I'm stressed out.

"I named him Macchiato, as in the coffee drink. I call him Mach for short, right boy?"

Mach the wolf-in-disguise thumps his tail while never removing his adoring gaze from Nate. Nate responds with a quick scratch behind the ears that are nearly as big as Nate's hands. Mach looks like a German shepherd, but much larger. Or maybe it's the proximity.

"That makes sense." I stare at Mach, unable to look at Nate. What was with the adolescent tongue-tiedness that suffocates me? As I look at Mach, take in his full gargantuan size, I also notice his sable coat. "Because of his coloring, right?"

"Exactly. He's like a dark shot of espresso topped with a dollop of froth."

Mach whimpers, his eyes imploring me. To leave him and his master alone?

"He wants you to pet him, but you don't have to."

"I'm more used to birds." I shoot him a quick smile and hope it isn't as pinched as it feels. "I have a parrot. Come here, Mach."

He eagerly closes the distance with two Mach steps, which are equivalent to twenty of mine. I pet his head and he twists to lick my hand before leaning his head full-bore into my hand, groaning in pleasure. I can't help it, I giggle.

"He's so soft. I've never met such a big German shepherd."

"He's a Shiloh shepherd. Think wolf appearance with a Labrador's temperament."

Mach proceeds to lay down and roll on his back for a belly rub. I comply, getting on my haunches and running my fingers through the soft white fluff. "Good boy, Mach."

"He likes you. But to be fair, he's affection-driven."

"I've been around a lot of dogs, but don't have one at the moment. I have my parrot, Ralph."

"Oh, I know you do. And you're a Navy pilot who's opening up an international curio shop."

"Retired Navy. And it's more than a curio shop. It's a cultural experience." Why can't I drop the know-it-all tone? It's not like—Oh crap. I've got the hots for the hottie. "Wait. How do you know all of this?"

His eyebrow raises in an expression of comic disbelief that tugs a serious belly laugh out of me. "It's Stonebridge. You grew up here, you should know. I've only been here six months, and everybody knows what DNA traits I carry by now."

"I've been back for almost as long. Sure, I'm from here, but I've been gone for a long time. What brings you here?"

He gives me a *really?* expression. *Caught.*

I hold up my hands in surrender. "I heard that you moved here from New York, to help out your parents."

"That's accurate by about fifty percent. It's my Mom I'm helping out, as she takes care of my Dad. They live on the other side of the block. My backyard backs up to theirs." He motions to my almost-house—his house—with his thumb. "This one's mine."

"I considered buying this house, but my shop's building has two floors of living space above it. It's the better choice for my situation." I'm a little disconcerted that we both liked the same house.

His expression sobers. "I'm sorry about what happened in your shop. Everyone in town is still in shock."

"Thanks. Me, too. Frannie is, was, a big part of Stonebridge. She and Ken have been pillars, I guess you could say." No matter that they'd had trouble in their marriage. Life happened to everyone. So did death, but no one deserved to be murdered in cold blood.

"When are you opening your store?"

"The original plan was Small Business Saturday, Thanksgiving weekend."

"You can still do that, then. It's over a week away."

"Yes, but…" But I can't get the image of Frannie's corpse out of my mind. And I don't think customers will, either.

Awkward silence stretches and I toe the cold pavement, the neon pink running shoes I thought were a great idea seeming juvenile considering the conversation's grave turn.

"I hope you can let what happened in your shop go enough to enjoy your grand opening. Again, I'm sorry that Mach startled you. We'll let you get back to your run."

"Oh, I don't run anymore. More like fast walk."

"Your next coffee's on me and Mach." He gives me a wave. Mach stares at me, and I wonder if he's a birder.

Too soon, girlfriend. How can I be jumping to Mach meeting Ralph right now?

"Thanks."

I walk on and wonder if Nate's watching me. But when I

turn to look, he and Mach have disappeared. I lengthen my stride, eager to get back to the shop, as if Nate's good wishes have rekindled my enthusiasm, made the specter of Frannie's murder a little dimmer.

Chapter Fifteen

"RALPH! WHERE ARE you?" It's Tuesday night and I cannot be late for the Stonebridge Buddies meeting. This is so not the time for my pickle-green parrot to hide. And it's unusual, this time of year. We're getting closer to the shortest day of the year, when Ralph's birdie hormones are calmest. Unlike when the light grows longer in spring and I risk a skin-breaking bite every time I pick him up. Hence, his handheld T-perch.

"Pretty bird, come on out." The Buddies are meeting in fifteen, no, make that twelve, minutes. It's only a five-minute walk to the coffee shop where we convene in the upstairs room, but the last thing I want is to be late to my first meeting when I've blown off attending for almost half a year.

I've had a long day in the shop, trying to get back on my planned timeline for the shop's opening, only ten more days away. I'm absolutely not in the mood to play hide-and-seek with a hormonal Yellow Nape Amazon parrot.

Ralph's not under the baker's rack, or on the top of it. He hasn't taken himself to the perch in my room, or the back of the sofa, two of his favorite spots as they allow him a window spot.

"*Uuuuuueeeetch!*" His scream makes me jump and for a split second I'm mentally in the shop storage room, Frannie's unseeing eyeballs swizzled with the glass sticks. Ugh.

I stomp into the bathroom, spy him atop the shower door, and hold the T-perch to his breast. "Step up, Ralph." He complies as trained since we rescued him.

"What's going on with you, bird?" I force myself to calm down and walk him to his cage, careful to not hit his head on the door as I maneuver the stick to where he can easily step onto his heated perch.

"Bye-bye." His farewell voice is sad, plaintive. Tears well, and I swipe at them before remembering I've put mascara on.

"It's okay, bud. I'll be back in a flash." I hope I will, that this meeting won't take longer than an hour or so. We all own business in Stonebridge, and it's the busiest time of year for retail. No one wants to stay out that late, do they?

"WE'RE ALL IN mourning over the loss of our colleague Frannie Schrock. As soon as we celebration of life details from Ken, we'll put it on the email loop. I know it's not the best timing to have this meeting, but Frannie would want—" Frederick "Red" MacIntosh stops his opening remarks and stares at me. I heard the meeting come to order as I climbed the steep stairs between the coffee shop retail floor and the community room. Latte Love occupies a nineteenth century building and its sheer enormity isn't obvious downstairs while sipping a café au lait. But up here, the ceiling reaches it full cathedral proportions, the gothic-shaped windows revealing the entire Main Street through wavy antique glass. The view tonight is pitch black, the harsh reflection the room's fluorescent lighting stark.

No less than thirty pairs of eyes drill their gazes into my soul as I search for an open seat. They're all seated around several wheeled tables that have been shoved together to form an impressive conference table. I walk toward the few remaining folded chairs against the back wall, but my hands are full. With no place to set the cup of chamomile I'd bought downstairs, I face an older man with a hairline that receded when Nixon was president. I don't recognize him and realize I don't know most of the people in the room. Another reminder that I've been gone a long time.

"Excuse me, could you please hold this for a sec?" I smile. He refuses to meet my gaze but takes the cup.

"Angel Warren. Welcome." Red's recovered his poise and I offer a quick nod as I sit down and lean over to retrieve the hot tea. "Sorry I'm late."

"The Buddies are known for our promptness, aren't we?" Red gets a murmur of agreement. Something starts to heat in my gut and I don't know if it's embarrassment or something less innocuous. I notice several people are still shooting me the death stare, and no less than four pairs lean into one another and whisper something or other.

So much for a warm welcome.

"Angel, Marjorie is the chair for our hospitality committee. You can get with her after the meeting is adjourned." Red smiles at Marjorie, his wife. Like Frannie and Ken, they've been together since high school. Red made his success in a combined business of studio photography and graphic design, while Marjorie runs an interior design business.

"Thank you."

Red is a solid leader and gets through the agenda that I printed out in my office in short order. That is, Red appears as eager as I am to get through the list of topics. The business owners around the table, not so much. Each one has an opinion on everything, or a need to express why a particular issue affects them more than anyone else at the table.

Settled in my seat, I take advantage of the spot in the back to go around the room, figure out who everyone is.

Nico's in the center of the side opposite me, and his wink bolsters my spirit. Next to him is Eloise, who spends a lot of time talking about how the laundromat next to hers disturbs the "energy flow" of her practices. Next to her is Gus Fisher, who owns Gus's Guitars where Jenna claims she was supposed to meet Frannie on Saturday. Gus—long, lean, and grisly with the hair and beard to match—is not a little bit of a cliché and I wonder if he reeks of pot. Weed isn't something that was ever an issue in the Navy, with its zero-tolerance policy on all drugs except alcohol. As a pilot, booze is off-limits for very specific periods of time prior to any mission. But things are different in Pennsylvania, where we're on the cusp of legalizing recreational use and medical cannabis prescriptions are not uncommon.

Red gets to the end of the printed agenda, and without fanfare concludes the meeting for "the real discussions." I stay in my seat, wondering how quickly I can escape.

No running. Frannie's murderer may be here.

"Hi, Angel, how's Ralph doing? Loved your Facebook post." Dana Slaughter stands in front of me. She and her wife own Cumberland Exotics, a pet store specializing in all animals aquatic, reptilian, and avian.

"Thanks. The one with him looking out the window?"

She laughs. "Yeah, the person walking by on the street looked so surprised!"

"It was a lucky shot. I was trying to get him, the store window, and the streetlight decoration in the same pic. It would have made a beautiful Christmas ad, until the woman wheeling her laundry down the sidewalk nearly jumped out of her wool coat and boots when Ralph screamed *hello* at the top of his lungs."

Dana looks around the room, takes an empty chair. Most folks are gathered around a festive table I didn't notice at first. It's heavy with sweat treats and a large urn of coffee. That should have been my first clue that these meetings, or the after-meetings, usually go long. Nothing like sugar and caffeine to keep things moving.

"Hey, um, how are you doing? Really? Claudia and I have been wondering. It had to have been awful to find someone like that."

"I'm okay, really, but thanks for asking. It's a tragedy."

"Not great for your business, either." Her sage nod makes my heart plummet. "Are you still going to open Thanksgiving weekend?"

"I plan to, yes." Guilt tries to creep in but I mentally bat it away. Frannie was all about business. "Frannie never wanted more than for Stonebridge to be successful."

"You're right. But can I be honest?" Dana's either not really listened or intent to rock my precarious sanity. "Rumors are floating that you did it."

"Why would I want Frannie dead?" I hear my voice raise and want to kick myself. I don't look but don't need to—I know the others heard. "She was my friend, since high school. The only thing connecting me to her murder is that it happened in my shop."

"If you need anything, Claudia and I are here for you."

"Thanks."

"One more thing. I know it sounds crass, but did Ralph—"

"Yes, Ralph was in the store. I'm going to check out the snack table. Tell Claudia hello for me."

I've no interest in any of the food, and caffeine this late

isn't my gig, either. But I take a look at what all the fuss is about, with nearly all the Stonebridge Buddies gathered round the goodies. No one notices me this time, as their backs are to me and I slip in near the coffee urn. I'm happy to spot a thermos carafe with a hot water tag alongside a serving tray of tea bags and help myself. Two things strike me. One, Dana's right. This town does think I had something to do with Frannie's demise. And two, how do they not think I can hear them? They're speaking in low tones, in groups of three or four, but we're in a closed room for heaven's sake.

"It's a damn shame that it's all ended this way…"

"I've no idea but I'll bet Angel does…"

"You never know someone, do you?"

"It's strange, is all I'm saying, coming back here of all places after what's supposed to have been a successful military career. Does that ring true to you?" Nadine Stolz, owner of Stolz's Spa and Respite, issues the last, her over-bleached hair in one of those sloppy buns that would never pass muster on a ship.

You're not at sea, you're in Stonebridge. A civilian.

A civilian who needed to stand up for herself.

"Excuse me?" I'm dunking my tea bag as calmly as I can, hoping to convey that none of their gossip is getting to me. I wait for all of them to look at me. "I'm sorry to burst in on your break, and I really am sorry for being late tonight." I decide to leave Ralph out of it. "Do any of you have any questions for me? It's my first Buddies meeting and I'm sure you may be wondering what made me pick an international curio shop as my second career."

I squish the last of the hot water out of the full bag and toss it into the trash. It makes a satisfying *plop* as it lands on discarded paper plates.

Complete—I mean dead, nil, nada, zip—silence blankets me and it's tempting to turn and leave. Swear off the Stonebridge Buddies and the horses they all didn't ride in on. Or worse, keep talking. Instead, I wait.

Tick, tick, tick. The plain Jane round clock on the wall reminiscent of elementary school is the only sound. I wonder what's going to happen first—a spoken word or a fart?

"You have to understand, Angel, we're all in complete shock. Nothing like this happens in Stonebridge." Red is the first to recover, his skin matching his nickname.

"Yes, what Red says." Drew Ashford, CPA, nods with such vigor it reminds me of the bobbing head Chihuahua my grandmother kept on the back window of her '77 Chevy Impala, right next to the tissue box with the neon crochet granny square cover. "We're all stunned. And it was in your building, after all."

"You can't blame us for being curious, Angel." Susan Packer crosses her arms in front of her most ample bosom. She owns Heavenly Lingerie, and it's hard to resent a woman who donates so much to breast cancer survivors. When my mother had a partial mastectomy, she got the inside scoop on all that Susan provides the community, especially women whose income wouldn't otherwise afford necessary items such as post-surgical drainage vests, pillows and custom bras. But saint or not, Susan appeared to be siding with the rest of the crowd who placed the blame for Frannie's death on me.

"Hold on a minute, everybody. Let's give Angel a chance to speak." Allie Davis, owner of Suds and Sparkles, a vegan bath shop that sells my favorite rose-scented lotion bath bomb, steps forward. Her long black locks hang straight, contrasting with the sage-and-red hand-knit sweater she's wearing. I know she's a knitter, as Bryce and Nico have mentioned how talented she is. And if she purchased such a beautiful piece, it'd be way out of her income's reach. Small business retailers don't net a whole lot in the first year or two, especially in an off-the-beaten-trek town like Stone-bridge.

"Thank you, Allie." I set my cup of tea in between a platter of frosted mitten cookies and mini-pumpkin pies. Using every ounce of public speaking skill I have, I make eye contact with each and every person before I continue. Only two look away, which I consider a win in a room of thirty or more.

"I understand why you might think I'd have something to do with Frannie's murder. I mean, it happened in my shop—"

"And your knickknacks were the murder weapons!" A deep male voice that I'm unable to place but it came from where the bald dude from earlier stands.

"Shut up, Ike!" Nico's imperious tone is a first, and I suppress a smile.

"Actually, no, my merchandise isn't what killed Frannie. I can't say what did, as the coroner is determining that." I'm not going to risk mentioning Trinity, or what she told me. The last thing I need is for a Stonebridge Buddy to get back to her before I do. She's going to be upset enough with me when she finds out I'm doing my own digging.

"What I do know is that the killer took those items, which were broken decorations, and placed them in such a way as to implicate me in the crime. Now, for those who don't know me, I'm Angel Warren, retired Navy pilot. I've finished up my Navy stint after twenty-two years and returned to Stonebridge because there's no place I'd rather be. I've lived in some wonderful places over the years, trust me. I've also served in combat and have seen enough tragedy to last a lifetime. Do you really think I'd move back here after all the places I've lived, just to kill one of our own?"

Not. One. Sound.

I nod. "Okay, so hear me out. Someone wanted Frannie dead, and tried to pin it on me. It's in my best interest to find the killer sooner than later, as my business opening is less than two weeks away. Small Business Saturday. Which means it's in *all* of our interest to find the killer. I need your help."

A few murmurs of—dare I say—agreement, a cough, two

sneezes.

"I'm not claiming to be working in an official capacity, but I'd appreciate the opportunity to speak with most if not all of you over the next couple of days. I promise to turn anything I find out, or piece together, over to SPD immediately. I'm not Perry Mason; I'm a Navy veteran who wants to continue to give back, at the local level."

"I think we can all get behind Angel, right folks?" Red all but hip-checks me out of the way as he takes the stage beside me. He gives me a broad smile that reveals bits of red and white between his teeth. Red's been enjoying the cookies sprinkled with crushed candy canes.

"Thank you. I'll be in touch with many of you, and I look forward to getting to know everyone better."

The crowd disperses into several different klatches, many according to the type of business they run, or maybe their commercial building's proximity to another's. It's hard to tell. Since there are many gathered, though, it's a perfect chance to get to knock out some of my questions about Frannie's murder. Why not? I've already created quite the stir. Annoying anyone further than I already have seems impossible.

I take a couple more cookies and head over to a wizened man I place somewhere between fifty and seventy-five, wearing a worn brimmed suede hat.

"Gus?"

He peers up from his cup of coffee and nods. "Evening,

Angel."

"How have you been?"

"Since you quit breaking E strings or more recent?" His grin spreads as wide as my relief. Gus doesn't think I killed Frannie. "I'm good."

"Still running your shop."

"A-huh. And before you ask, yes, Frannie's assistant was in my shop on Saturday afternoon." He winks. "Detective Colson beat you to it."

"I'm sure she did. I'm not trying to do her job, you know."

"I don't see it as a problem if you are. Like you said, more hands involved, the sooner we put this senseless tragedy behind us."

A gavel sounds on its leather pad and I turn to see Red back at the front of the room.

"Thanks, Gus. Talk to you later."

We retake our seats and Red resumes with the planned agenda. It's a small step, finding out that Jenna's alibi is solid. There are so many unanswered questions competing for attention it's hard to focus on Red. Once I do, I feel like I've come home.

No one's jumping up and down for a chance to talk to me, but for the first time since I walked into Latte Love tonight, I have what I've been missing since Frannie died.

Hope.

Chapter Sixteen

"NO, NO, H-E-DOUBLE hockey sticks no!" Trinity's standing in the middle of the store, hands on hips. She's wearing civilian clothes, but there's no mistaking the large weapon holstered on her hip under the houndstooth blazer. It's still early Wednesday morning, but she looks like she's been up for hours. Maybe she has.

"I don't know what you heard, but hold on." I put the last few Christmas elves in place on the shelf adjacent the Russian Santa display. The elves are hand-felted in Azerbaijan and are bedecked in brilliant hues of fuchsia, aquamarine, and violet. What I loved about collecting decor from around the globe was the cultural take each region gave to traditional Western European and North American holidays. The elves are definitely elves, and their red-and-green stocking hats and socks shout "Christmas," but the fabric choices are definitely not traditional. "Okay, let me guess. You found out about the Stonebridge Buddies meeting."

"Dang straight. Why on earth would you think for one second that you should be involved in a murder investigation? Not just Frannie's, but any criminal investigation?"

Trinity's as unhinged as I'd thought she'd be, and I'm mad at myself for not going to her first.

"I'm not playing detective. And I'll tell you anything I hear." I motion for her to follow me back to my office. Once there, I motion at the coffee and tea station I set up. "Can I get you anything? Or better, please help yourself. I've got some snacks left over from the Buddies meeting."

"I didn't come here to chitchat, Angel." But I see her gaze longingly land on a clear plastic bowl of homemade holiday cereal mix. "Oh, all right. Where are the napkins?"

"There." I point to the neat stacks of paper napkins and plates, imprinted with snowmen and turkeys. "We're definitely between seasons. Do you want tea or coffee? And I have bottled water, too."

"Tea, please." Trinity snorts as she picks out savory tidbits. "They put up the Christmas decorations on the streetlights before most people have bought their turkey for Thanksgiving."

"I know." I put the electric kettle on to boil and grab more of the mitten-shaped cookies. I already ate three last night.

"You've never lost your sweet tooth, I see."

"No. And I still envy your stick-thin figure because you prefer salty."

"You can't blame extra pounds on just sugar. Although, you're taking good care of yourself."

I sigh. "Usually I'm a lot better at self-control around the sweets, but this time of year is difficult." Especially in the midst of a very stressful time, surrounded by all the comforts from my childhood. "I don't dare let myself buy a box of spiced wafers at the grocery store."

Trinity takes a seat on one of the two folding chairs I've set out in front of my desk. I pour the water into the mugs and take the second seat, placing our mugs and a basket of assorted teabags on the desk. "Help yourself to whatever tea you like."

"You still work out?" She picks English Breakfast, and I take Earl Grey.

"Yes. Mostly walking, and I've done yoga classes on base, before. I suppose I need to sign up for classes with Eloise. Her studio sure is conveniently located. I haven't had time to do anything but put the store together since the girls went off, and now, with, you know..." I'm reluctant to mention Frannie as we're enjoying a bit of solid companionship. Searching for a distraction, dunk my tea bag a few times.

She nods. "I do know. And I know you, Angel. Sure, we've been out of touch for a long while, but we wouldn't be able to sit here like this if we didn't still click. Which is why I'm asking you, as a friend, to mind your own business. Worry about setting up your shop. I'll take care of the murderer."

A chill runs over my nape, across my forearms. "My brother and his husband think I'm nuts to stay in the building until you catch him."

"We're keeping a good eye on it."

"Any suspects?"

"You know I can't discuss details. But this looks a lot like what I saw in Harrisburg. The demographics are different, sure, but whoever did this caught Frannie in your shop instead of you. They were looking for easy cash."

"And didn't realize how valuable some of my stock is." Other than my desk being ransacked, the locked bottom drawer forced open and dumped, there were no other signs of a search for money or valuables.

"I know that you have some expensive items in here, but unless it's a computer or gun, forget it. An addict wants a quick sale, quick cash."

"So you think it was a heroin addict?" I'd read about the opioid epidemic. It basically tore through central Pennsylvania like an evil, twisted tornado, leaving devastation in the form of bereaved families in its wake. And it wasn't over.

She shrugs. "Heroin, prescription pills, you name it."

"Your job is hard. I'd never want it."

"Good. Then we agree that you'll stick to setting up shop?"

"Well, it can't hurt if I talk to folks, can it? And of course I'll report anything I find out to you."

Her brows draw together. "This is what I'm talking about, Angel. You say *report* as if you work for me, and you don't. You're not on the case, or mission, or whatever you called it in the Navy."

"But you can't fault me, Trinity. It's my property where Frannie was killed. Did you know that most of the small business owners believe I did it? I explained myself at the Stonebridge Buddies meeting, but you know how stubborn the folks around here are. That hasn't changed since we left high school."

"No, it hasn't. But what has is that they're getting a little more accepting. Two different sources told me about your request for information."

I stop, mid-cookie bite. "You've gotten flack for being the first female lead detective of SPD?"

She rolls her eyes. "Hello. Yes, of course, but we both know what they're most upset about."

"You're Black."

"Yes indeed-y." Trinity's expression is resigned, but not in the *I can't change them* way. More like, *they're going to learn to deal with it.*

"I'm proud of you. You've accomplished so much, Trinity. You're the bravest person I know."

"Keep talking." She waits a long beat before flashing me a bright smile. "Hey, I'm not doing anything no one else is. Giving it my all, getting it done."

"Well, I'm grateful you agreed to take this position. Your expertise is invaluable with this case, I'm sure."

"Stop blowing smoke, Angel." She doesn't finish it, but we both know it's *up my butt.* I giggle. "You are not Nancy Drew or 007."

"More like Inspector Clouseau?"

She methodically wipes her fingers with the turkey napkin, purses her lips. I know better than to say a word.

"You're going to do what you're going to do. But hear me out. You're a civilian, even with your military background. Unless you have some kind of police training I'm unaware of?"

I shake my head. "No."

"Okay. Do you carry a weapon, have one in your home?"

"You know I don't." SPD had searched every inch of the building, and I have never applied for a gun license.

"So you have no protection against a hardened criminal, a murderer, who is still out there."

"No. But you said yourself that you think it wasn't personal, it was a drug-related crime. What are the odds they're still hanging around?" I don't happen to agree with Trinity on the drug-related deal. Sure, it looks like it, but there was something so sinister, so very personal about the Santa stake to Frannie's heart, the swizzles to her eyes. I can't shake that this crime is more than a random try for quick cash.

"That's for me and my team to figure out."

"But if you're wrong, and the murderer is someone more local, wouldn't it make sense to have someone on the ground, collecting whatever information comes up?"

"Sure. Except what will you do if the murderer decides they don't want you nosing around?"

Chapter Seventeen

T RINITY AND I leave it at *we agree to disagree.* With a solid, pinkie-swear promise that I tell her anything and everything I might happen to come up with, if and only if it comes my way naturally.

Have I mentioned that a Navy motto is *better to beg forgiveness than ask for permission*?

Which is why only hours later I'm smack dab in the middle of Suds and Sparkles listening to Allie expound upon the benefits of vegan lotions, bath bombs, bath salts, soaps, and lip scrubs. Allie Davis opened her store just under a year ago, before I moved back. But the airy, open space is chock full of enticing displays in what has to be every possible floral scent imaginable. There's a kid's corner, too, that boasts smaller containers and golf-ball-sized bath bombs in popular kid food scents. Chocolate cupcake, vanilla frosting, and cheese-y crackers are only a few.

"Each bath bomb has no less than five grams of coconut oil infused with sarsaparilla essence, which is why we call it our root beer float." Allie tilts her head and presents one of the sparkling molded balls in her hand as if it's a precious gem. "The food-safe glitter floats on top of your bath, and drains with zero harm to your plumbing." I'm admiring her festive clothing, again. Today's sweater is a charcoal-gray cardigan with snowman buttons and a red-and-white fair isle patterned yoke. I recognize the pattern as one of Bryce's and say so.

"Yes, I took his color work class last year. Here, check this out." She shoves the bath bomb under my nose.

I sniff. "Wow, that's incredible. It really does smell like root beer!"

She nods. "Sure does." She opens her mouth to continue and I see my tactical window.

"Allie, at the Stonebridge Buddies meeting you mentioned that this past Saturday you were having a make-it-yourself drop-in event?" I've never been accused of being a tact master.

Her head twerks to her right, her gaze sharpens. "Yes. Frannie's assistant Jenna was here, as a matter of fact. The police questioned me about it already. That's why you're in my store, right?"

Dang.

"Partially, yes. I also need more of your custom bath balm bombs. My bathtub is the only way I can relax these days." I'm not above greasing the inquisition wheels.

"Well, I sure hope you have a crowbar handy, or a baseball bat. There's a murderer on the loose!" She lowers her voice on the last. "I'm keeping Romeo with me, in the back, at all times until they catch them."

"Romeo?"

"You don't know Romeo?" She points to a table I haven't visited yet. A Pitbull-shaped cutout sports the prices of doggie shampoo, doggie conditioner, and natural peanut butter flavored doggie dental paste. "He's my inspiration. Come on back and meet him." She nods to a woman standing behind the counter. I guesstimate she's the same age as the twins.

"Watch the store, Courtney." as she lifts the top and ushers me to the other side.

"Will do." Courtney's bright eyes and aura of exuberance, so much like Ava and Lily, trigger the longing I've struggled to keep tamped down. I miss my girls so much.

We go through a small door into an area larger than the storefront. Stoves and presses and workspaces galore compete for space. A long wall of dowels holds myriad stickers, labels for the varying tins, bottles, and jars that hold the merchandise. I'm impressed by the neatness, the lack of any one overwhelming scent.

"Kudos to you, Allie. Your products are never too strong, scent-wise."

"Oh, that's another reason to choose all-natural products. If it's going to touch your skin, why would it need to be a strong scent?"

I can think of when my body needs a stronger-than-BO-aroma, like after a long day in an airplane or, say, after

GERI KROTOW

finding a corpse. But I keep my observation private. I'm here to build bridges, aid the community, and catch a killer. Not antagonize a possible informant.

Allie leads us behind a large stainless-steel work counter to reveal a powder blue fluffy dog bed with the most beautiful dog sitting up on it.

"Oh, we woke him up!" Romeo blinks once, twice, all the while regarding me with steady, sorrowful amber eyes.

"This is Romeo. Romeo, meet Angel." Romeo's bottom wriggles.

"What a dear! Can I pet him?"

"Yes, please. I do all I can to socialize him. Take your time, though. He has a traumatic past." Allie smiles at her beloved canine. "Good dog, Romeo, it's okay. Angel's our friend."

I cautiously bend over and hold my hand out for the silver-coated canine. Romeo takes a few steps forward and sniffs before licking my fingers with his approval.

"Good doggie." I scratch behind his ears and remember much larger doggie ears from the other day. Nate's dog, Mach. I haven't seen him since then, not that I wish I had or that I've been thinking of him. The dog, not necessarily the owner.

"He's sweet, sure, but on my command he'll take down the murderer without hesitation."

"Sounds better than the alarm system I had installed on Monday!"

"Definitely. An alarm system only warns. Romeo's going to be with me 24/7 until the killer's in jail." Allie's shudder punctuates her fear, and the stark terror in her eyes contrasts with the cozy, self-care ambience of her shop. "I've moved back in with my folks, too. I don't want to live alone right now."

"I don't blame you." Allie can't be more than five years older than my girls. I'd want them with me, too, if they hadn't left town. "I'm impressed, Allie. By all accounts, Suds and Sparkles is booming. Have you always wanted to own your own business? And why did you pick bath products?"

"Yeah, so, I knew that owning my own business was my path, for sure. I sold all kinds of things as a kid, you know, for the school fundraisers?"

I nod as I continue to pet Romeo's soft fur.

"I studied business in high school, and went to HACC."

"HACC has it all, doesn't it? I've thought of taking some business classes there myself." Harrisburg Area Community College is more than what community college was when I graduated high school. Many of the twins' friends have enrolled at HACC for everything from nursing to premed.

"HACC is great, I must say. I was going to get my MBA next, but when my grandmother died, she left me with enough cash to start Suds and Sparkles. I do still plan to get my MBA, however. As soon as I have enough reliable employees to man the shop, I'm going to attend a night or weekend program."

"Your parents must be so proud of you, Allie." And I mean it. Heck, I'm proud of her. And I hardly know her.

"They are. Mom works here on weekends, especially this time of year. I need all hands on deck!" I doubt she realizes she's used a Navy colloquialism, but it tugs at my pride nonetheless.

It describes my drive to solve Frannie's murder ASAP. It's an all-hands-on-deck situation, no question.

I give Romeo a final pat until I get to see him again and stand. "Thanks for showing me around, Allie."

"Of course! What kind of balm bomb did you want?"

"Lavender if you have it. And maybe a rose, too."

"I have both in stock. We've been making inventory for what feels like a century."

"For the holidays?"

"Yes. We're in production every week of the year, but the pre-orders and website sales have slammed us. In the best way, of course."

"You mentioned hiring was a problem? I'm going to need at least one other person to man the register, and I'm searching for an overall assistant to handle the website, social media, promo and store events." Basically I want a mini-me, for an affordable wage.

Allie's mouth tips in a semi-frown and she lets out a punctuated sigh. "I wish I could tell you not to worry about it, but I've had so much turnover this past year it'd make your head spin. Every business in town has the same problem."

"Is it the hourly wage issue?" I know that most local businesses can't compete with the national chains, of which there are an abundance in the Harrisburg Area, all within twenty minutes of Stonebridge.

"That, and the younger crowd wants benefits that I know I for one can't afford."

"What kind of benefits?"

"Scholarships, for one. The local grocery stores all have programs to help college students with tuition. Plus they pay, on average, two dollars and thirty-eight cents an hour more." Allie sure did her homework.

"I'll keep that in mind. To be honest, I've been swamped with getting ready for my grand opening."

Allie regards me with a sage gaze that belies her years. "And now you have to fight the rumor mill."

"By the way, I never thanked you properly for sticking up for me last night. I really appreciate it."

Her grin is instant. "Aw, it wasn't a big deal. The Buddies can be a bunch of diehard gasbags if you ask me. But talking to any of them one-on-one, they're really nice. A lot of them knew my grandparents."

"Still, you didn't have to speak up. You don't know me well. Why did you?"

"We're back to the real estate assistant question again, right? I told the police all I know, what I saw. Jenna came in here later in the morning, maybe an hour, hour-and-a-half after we opened."

I turn my head and confirm the hour by the numbers painted on her entrance door. "You opened at ten."

"Right. Jenna's a frequent flyer in here, so I recognized her right away."

"Did she seem any different to you?"

"Do you mean do I think she killed Frannie?" She laughs. "Of course not. Jenna was totally herself, very relaxed, quiet. She spent a lot of time at the bath salts." She motions to a counter at one side of the store that's laden with glass jars of salt blends. "That's how I know she couldn't have been in your store. Besides, Jenna's the kind of person who'd take a spider outside instead of stepping on it. I've known her since our Brownie troop trips."

"Thanks for letting me know, Allie. You're right—I'm not a cop, or anything at all near it. I just want people to know my shop had nothing to do with her death."

"I don't think anyone really believes that. The people here just need something to talk about."

"Is there anyone that you know has been particularly upset with Frannie recently?"

"Honestly, no. We all get, I'm sorry, got, tired of her obsession with making Stonebridge a true resort town. I think it's safe to say that most of us locals are happy with things as they are. Do we want more business? Of course! But that's what an online shop is for, if you ask me."

She rings up my order and packages it so prettily I know

I won't want to open it right away.

"Thank you, Allie. That's perfect!"

"Here's an idea for you. There's a bulletin board at the coffee shop, right when you walk in. They allow everyone to post whatever they want. You could make a flyer about needing help at your shop. It's how I've found almost all of my employees."

"Thanks. That's a great idea."

So what if this means I'll be going to Latte Love? It's not like I'm going there to catch a glimpse of Nate. This is purely business.

Chapter Eighteen

"SURE YOU DON'T want whipped cream on that?" Nate's courtesy is professional only, but it doesn't stop the flutters from tickling my ribcage. Said butterflies unfurled the minute I walked in and saw him steaming milk at the coffee machine.

"No, thanks. I ate my weight in cookies last night. When I was a kid, Christmas cookies weren't until Christmas Eve."

"That right?" He slides the peppermint mocha across the counter, and I see his latte art extends to snowmen. Except, it's a snow woman, with long hair.

"Nate, you have a real talent."

"Thanks, but seriously, anyone can learn to do it. I'm a left-brained guy but picked it up in the training our coffee supplier offers every month."

"What did you do, before?" The question pops out before I can turn off my inner Miss Marple.

"Engineering." He's vague and I take the hint, along with my coffee, as I turn to walk to a table.

"What kind of cookies?"

"Huh?"

"You said you had cookies last night. I'm a cookie aficio-nado. I just wondered."

Heat waves up my throat, my face. "Oh, um, it was here. Upstairs."

"You were at the Stonebridge Buddies meeting?"

"I was. Does that surprise you?"

"That you're a member, no. You own a local business. But it couldn't have been easy. I hope they weren't too hard on you."

"Meaning?"

He shrugs. "I sling coffee. I hear a lot. Folks are worried, is all. I wouldn't take it personally, about Frannie, that it happened in your building. Folks are just scared, is all. Fear does strange things to people." He's cleaning the milk frothers with a soft cloth, polishing the stainless-steel pipes to a bright shine that reflects the twinkling blue-and-white lights strung on the rectangular appliance. This part of the counter is the Hanukah section and my gaze catches on the hand-printed ceramic menorah atop the entire display. My fingers itch to take a peek and see where it was made.

"Something catch your eye?" His tone is light, as if he senses I need a change of topic.

"This menorah...where did you get it?"

"Amy's responsible for the decor in here. She's our store manager."

"I thought you ran the store?"

"I own it." Quietly stated.

"You weren't at the Stonebridge Buddies meeting last night." Or serving. I would have noticed.

"I was holed away in the back office, getting the books done. I don't attend all the meetings. As much as I enjoy the small-town life, I'm not all that interested in the politics, if you get my drift. I'm a Buddies member, and give them a free place to hold meetings."

"That's generous of you. Back to Amy, how has that worked for you, to have a manager? I'm actually here to put up help needed sign on your bulletin board."

"Please do. Having Amy has changed the game for me. As a business owner by definition my blood, sweat, and tears are invested, one hundred percent. But I know what I'm good at, and what's best left to experts. Amy's a driven worker who knows how to make things happen. I want to make coffee, meet my customers, and keep the doors open behind the scenes. Having a manager frees up my head space." He grins and the tension in my chest eases. No matter that half the town thinks I killed Frannie, Nate doesn't care, or if he does, he's not acting like he does. Having a complete—well, almost—stranger trust me is truly heartwarming.

Unless.

Unless it means Nate's the killer. I gulp. And start coughing, the latte somewhere in the vicinity of my tonsils.

"Here." He quickly fills a cup with water and slides it in front of me.

"Thanks." I gulp the cold liquid. "Nate, can I ask you a question?"

"Shoot." Does he pick this word for any reason?

"Where were you Saturday afternoon?"

"When Frannie was murdered." A statement, no frills.

"Yes."

He sets the cloth down, leans against the back counter. I don't allow myself to check out how his jeans fit snugly in the right places. Not while he's a possible suspect.

"I already explained myself to Detective Colson. Are you acting on her behalf, to catch me in some supposed lie, Angel Warren?" His tone is light but I hear the warning tone. I wish I could say the shivers on my spine are from fear but hey, I'm a warm-blooded woman.

"No, I'm definitely not acting in any official capacity, trust me. Trinity would have my hide in a blink. I'm asking for me, for my business that's not off the ground yet, and mostly, for Frannie."

He pushes off the work edge and takes the single step to bring him no more than a foot from me. "Then I have no problem assuring you that I was here the entire time. See that?" He points to elaborate cornice detail above the main entry.

"The carved lion?"

"Check out his mouth." Nate's breath is a blast of mint, not the gag-reflex coffee breath I'd expect. He does sip coffee behind the counter. Not that I watch him over much. My gaze follows his finger, and there, in between the roaring lion's sharp teeth, is a round lens.

"I never saw that before!"

"I had the entire place wired for security as soon as I signed on the dotted line to purchase. Not only does it add to my peace of mind, it's a great insurance discount."

"I'm doing the same."

"You won't regret it."

Nor will I regret the extra time with Nate.

Focus on solving Frannie's murder.

I am, but it's okay to enjoy a fun distraction, isn't it?

Sure, until the murderer sneaks up on you.

Since I'm sitting in Latte Love, I should speak to Sylvia's niece. I didn't notice her when I was talking to Nate but, well, Nate's a distraction onto himself. Just what kind of engineer was he?

Before I can type G-O-O-G-L-E into my keyboard I hear a familiar female voice. Amy's greeting a customer, taking an order. I bide my time, sip what's left of the peppermint mocha. Pumpkin spice is all the rage before Thanksgiving but not for me. I can drink Christmas concoctions year-round. Although for Christmas in July I do like to ice the peppermint mochas.

Another group of customers enter and impatience makes my face hot. But there's no sense trying to get any information out of Amy in front of a crowd. I need to know exactly what Frannie did to make Sylvia shutter the tea shop, and I doubt Amy or anyone else would be willing to speak publicly about anything to do with Frannie. I don't blame them.

Finally, Amy's alone at the counter, replenishing the glass case with individually wrapped slices of pumpkin cranberry bread.

Not for the first time I think about how silly this is. I'm basically creeping around town trying to extract information about a murder from people I don't know well, at least not yet. Except Frannie's death is the antithesis of silly.

"Amy?" I wait for her to look up from the large cartons of baked goods. She is slim but strong, her hands deliberate in placing each baked good in its proper place, making the display all the more enticing. The scent of butter, cranberry and pumpkin is distracting but sweets are the last thing I need.

"Yes?"

"I'm Angel. I'm the owner of Shop 'Round the World, down the street. I know your Aunt Sylvia. I hear she's moved to the shore last spring."

"Yes, she said you'd moved back here." She smiles. "We talk almost every day. She's more like my mother, to be fair. How's it going with the curio shop? Have you opened yet?" She peels off her latex gloves.

"Well, it's not a curio shop per se but an international gift shop of sorts." Marketing is not my strong point, have I mentioned that? "I'm opening in ten days." I hope.

She frowns. "It can't be easy, with Frannie being found there and all."

"No, it hasn't been. Can I ask you something?" I move closer to the counter, so that no one will overhear. Fortunately it's that lull in the afternoon between lunch and when the kids come in after school. The coffee shop's the least busy I've seen it.

"What's up?" Her long blonde hair is tied back in a ponytail and her gaze is direct.

"Do you happen to know the details about when Sylvia closed the tea shop?"

She leans back, crosses her arms over her chest, hiding the graphic tee that sports a half-eaten gingerbread cookie that says, BITE ME.

"I know the ins and outs of the tea shop's demise all too well. What do you want to know?"

"Why did she close up shop? It's just that my mother and sister and I used to love to get Christmas tea there every year, and I know we weren't alone. I've moved back after a long time away and it's sad to see the changes."

"It was a lot of things, to be fair. Aunt Sylvie's health hasn't been great. Mostly because she stresses too much over things she can't control. Schrock Real Estate's way of doing business was one of them."

"Oh?"

"I'm sure you already know this, but they're the biggest thing in Stonebridge, as far as commercial property goes.

They own at least half of the buildings. Three years ago Fr—Schrock Real Estate went on a rent-raising spree, especially along Main Street. It wasn't just our store that got it. Remember the tattoo parlor? And the dog groomer's? They're all gone, too. I know all of this because I worked in the tea shop over school breaks from college." Her obvious reluctance to mention Frannie's name doesn't strike me as grief driven.

"I just dropped my girls, twins, off at college. Pitt and Temple. Where did you go to school, Amy?" I give myself a mental pat on the shoulder for not interrogating her as I would a sailor.

"Penn State. Harrisburg campus for two years, then I transferred to State College."

"Great choice. What was your major?"

"Premed at first, but then I switched to Physical Therapy."

"What a good field to get into. PT has kept my shoulders in top shape over the years."

"Yeah, well, the plan was to finish up my PT certification right after. I only needed another eighteen months. But Aunt Sylvie, who paid for my college, couldn't afford to send me. Schrock has always owned our building, and the rent would raise here and there but nothing out of line."

"Did you think about taking out loans?"

"Sure did, but family comes first. Aunt Sylvie was beside herself trying to make ends meet. She overbooked events, didn't give herself enough recoup time in between high teas.

And you probably already know about the hiring issue, since I saw your flyer on the bulletin board. She needed my help but it wasn't enough. There was no way out for the tea shop. Aunt Sylvie doesn't have a pension from anywhere else. The tea shop's all she's ever had." Amy's defense of Sylvie hits me in the solar plexus. Is she inferring that opening my shop is easier because I have a Navy pension? Which is none of her business. Sure, I have healthcare and a pension for life, but it's not enough to support the girls through college, even after splitting my GI Bill with them. I force myself to let it go and focus on Amy.

"My sister told me she had to close the shop, but I had no idea how hard it was on Sylvie." Nor how complicated. My compassion for Amy wells. She's working here instead of going to graduate school as she'd planned, as Sylvia had planned. Frannie and Ken pulled the rug out from under them. Guilt follows quickly on empathy's heels. Frannie's not here to defend herself ever again.

"It's all worked out. Sylvie had a decent nest egg that I insisted she leave alone. I was so afraid she was going to draw from it for the shop, which would have been disastrous. This way she's in a nice little place outside of Cape May. She's thinking about opening a small tea place there."

"That sounds lovely, and Cape May is definitely a tea-lovers destination. Do you get there a lot?"

"Not this time of year. I worked there all summer and put away a good amount. I'm back here until next May. I live with my cousin so it's a decent setup. Now that Aunt

Sylvie's settled, I'm applying to start grad school next fall."

"Good for you!"

She shrugs. "Yeah. You're asking me all this because why?"

"Just new and finding my way around here. And like I said, I know your Aunt Sylvie. She's more familiar with my mother, of course. Please tell her we send our best."

"I will. Do you happen to need a store manager?"

"Not yet, but after hearing Nate sing your praises, I'm thinking it might not be a bad idea. Right now I'm looking for someone to handle my social media promo, some event planning."

"I'm free most nights. If you don't need me in the store itself during retail hours, I'd be interested."

"Aren't you already full-time here?" The last thing I want to do is poach Nate's top employee.

"I'm saving for grad school. I'll take all the hours I can get, anywhere."

"Let me think about it." Meaning, I need to talk to Nate about it. "Thanks for your time, Amy."

"Sure thing."

I walk out of Latte Love with my head spinning. And it's not about Shop 'Round the World, which needs my total attention. Is it possible that Amy harbors a deep, dark resentment against Frannie over Sylvie's early retirement? Strong enough to not only kill, but to make it look like I did it?

Chapter Nineteen

THE NEXT DAY, exactly one week before Thanksgiving, I stay in the store all morning, finally in a mental place to get some work done. The question of who killed Frannie continues to distract me, but until I work up some nerve I'm not going to get any further.

I need to go talk to Ken again, but not as a sympathy visit. I want to know what his role in raising the rents was. Frannie is taking the visible hit from all I've heard, but it's Schrock Real Estate, as in, Frannie *and* Ken. My mind wants to wander down the righteous path of feminist theory, how women have always been blamed for whatever throughout history. It shouldn't surprise me that outgoing, assertive Frannie had attracted the resentment of many Stonebridge Buddy members.

The bells on the store entrance ring and I look over at my tablet to see who it is. The security system is indeed top-notch and allows me to view all the building entrances, no matter where I am in the world, via an app. I immediately recognize the tall, white-haired figure and leave my desk.

"Dad! What a nice surprise." I walk to him and we hug.

The scent of late autumn along with the unusual cold clings to him, almost overpowering his Old Spice. I look him over. He cuts a handsome profile and has never met a piece of clothing that doesn't look perfect on him. Today he's covered a burgundy cashmere pullover with his scarf and slate-blue all-weather jacket. "What's going on?"

"What, I need a reason to visit my lovely daughter on a fine afternoon?"

"No, but you must have one. You've never been in here unless I've invited you."

"Well maybe you should invite me more." He erases any sense of hard feelings with his wide grin. I know it's a match to mine. I got my mother's hair and eyes. Dad's gene pool gets credit for my mouth and square jaw. Both girls have his smile, too.

"Come on back and get a cup of coffee. Or we can walk up to Latte Love?"

He waves away my offer with a sputter. "No thanks. That froufrou coffee's not for me, you know that."

I grin to myself as I turn and make my way to the beverage station.

"Take my chair."

"Naw, I'll sit here. That's your spot." He nods at my specialty desk chair and sits on one of the cushioned folding chairs. "Do you have any decaf? Your mother will want to know what I had and I hate to lie to her."

"Sure do. Give me a minute." I turn on the kettle and

reach for the single-serve French press. "I bought this decaf blend the other day I think you'll like."

"Coffee's coffee. I hope you're making me instant."

"Close enough." I lean my hip against the high counter, waiting for the water to boil.

"Looks like you've gotten a lot accomplished." His gaze moves to the entrance to the storage room. I get it; the draw is a primal thing. As if the deepest part of our brain needs to see exactly where the murder happened, so that we can prevent it from happening to us.

"You mean considering a murder happened last weekend?"

"Is it already almost a week?" He scratches his chin. "I'll tell you, since I retired my sense of time has flown the coop."

I pour the water for our drinks and take the seat next to him. "You don't wish you were still working?" Dad had been the town's single CPA for years, and then two other accountants set up their offices.

"Sometimes, sure, I miss the people, helping folks out with their numbers. You'd be surprised how many business owners avoid balancing their books in any form."

"Before I started this new venture, I might have been surprised that anyone would avoid something as big as financial accountability. But now that I'm working to get the store open, I understand why it's easy to push the books to the back of the line. There's so much else that needs to be done."

"Yeah, well, the taxman still has to get paid. Don't miss your quarterly taxes and you'll never go wrong."

"I won't. And if you decide you don't want to do my books, I'm more than happy to ask one of the other CPAs in town."

"I'm happy to do it. I want to do it. You and a few other people are my remaining clientele. It keeps my brain exercised and gives me something to do when I can't get out."

"How was it today? A personal best?" I hand him his coffee.

"Thank you." He wraps his hands around the warm mug. "Nothing to report. It was too cold to stay out there longer than nine holes."

"But still, Dad, you were outside for almost two hours, right?"

"Something like that." He sips. His brows shoot up toward his silver hairline. "Whoa. This isn't bad."

"It's from Latte Love. I told you we could have gone there. It's more comfortable than these seats." I keep dunking my tea infuser. The Irish Breakfast tea's aroma competes with Dad's coffee in the small space.

"And pay those prices, for a coffee? No thanks."

I laugh. "I would have treated, Dad."

"Ah, well." He's stalling. Dad never hesitates to treat any of us to whatever he can. More like what we'll allow him to do.

I know my Dad. He was the one who held me up

through Tom's funeral, took the girls to check out colleges when my schedule couldn't handle the extra load. How many active-duty persons have a parent they can rely on as much, to send their teen-aged kids over the pond (Atlantic Ocean) to their grandparents for college visits? He's got that concerned glint in his eyes that he's trying to cover up with lighter banter. "Are you still aiming for Small Business Saturday for your grand opening?"

"Yes. It's hard to believe it's only a little over a week away."

"That's what doing something you love does for you. I never thought twice about tax season. People always wonder how CPA's get through it but for me, it was never a grind. I always worked better under pressure."

"I remember that. Mom made us take turns fixing dinner while she graded the senior papers." April was when Mom, a high school English teacher, set the deadline for the assignments. She said it was in case any had to be rewritten. "She did that so that she didn't miss you as much."

"Maybe." He scratched his chin. "Your mother sent me in here."

"I knew it." I said it without alacrity. "She's not going to stop until the killer is caught."

"Can you blame her? Honey, we're worried." He held up his hands when I opened my mouth to reply. "Hang on. We know you can take care of yourself. You've been in combat. But you don't know what you're dealing with here. This murder was cold-blooded when I read between the lines of the news reports."

"Dad, you can't believe everything in print." Although the local paper was very, very good. I'd refrained from giving any of my family too many details. Bryce and Nico promised to keep whatever I'd blurted out on Saturday night to themselves. I'd still been in shock. Trinity was adamant that the fewer people who knew what I'd seen, the better. Now that I was determined to help find the killer I didn't want any privileged information to get out, either.

"I know that, honey."

"And look." I got up and grabbed the tablet, turned it to face him. "I knew it was you who walked in the door the minute you did. If you were a stranger, or someone concerning, I would have pushed this button and the police would be here—oh, shoot!"

I'd inadvertently tapped on the 911 button. My fingers flew over the glass surface to cancel the mistake, but it was too late.

"911, what's your emergency?"

"There isn't an emergency. I'm sorry, I pressed the call button by mistake." I cast a quick look at my Dad. His brow was up. He was worried about me, but also impressed with this system.

"I'm going to need to verify your identity. Please answer your cell phone."

My phone rang before she finished, and I picked it up. As soon as I finished the call, I set both devices back on my desk.

"I have to admit, that was straight out of a science fiction novel."

"No, it's reality, Dad. I'm safe."

"Except most killers know their victims, and vice versa. There's a good chance you won't be afraid of the murderer when they show up, because they'll be the last person you suspect."

"Dad, you and Mom have to lay off the BBC police dramas."

"Poppycock."

We both laughed. The doorbells jingle and I looked to see who it was.

"Oh boy."

"What?" Dad stood, his stance nothing less than Clint Eastwood material.

Before I answered, Trinity walked into the office. She looked me up and down, then scrutinized my Dad, the entire office, the back storage room.

"So you really are okay?"

"Yes. I'm so, so sorry. I won't make that mistake again. The tablet is far more sensitive than I realized."

"Didn't you work with more advanced technology in the Navy?"

"In the aircraft, sometimes, yes. But usually?" I shook my head. "We're years, sometimes decades behind the commercial world."

"Huh. Hey, Mr. Strooper. Good to see you."

"Is it appropriate for me to give a Stonebridge Detective a hug?" Dad opened his arms wide and Trinity doesn't hesitate. After their embrace, she smiled at Dad.

"A hug from you is always welcome. Just don't reach for my weapon and we're good." She turned to me. "I'm glad you sprung for the higher-end security system. For the record, I knew you were safe and that they'd validated it, but with something as odd as a murder in Stonebridge, I felt better checking it out myself."

"I appreciate it. Dad's here on a mission from Mom because they're both worried about me staying upstairs."

"Mr. Strooper, I'd be worried, too, if it were my child. But my department is keeping an eagle eye on this building, and you just saw for yourself how well the security system works. Angel's safe. If I thought any differently, I'd be camping out here myself."

"Thank you."

"You would?" I was happy that Trinity and I were getting our friendship back on track but still wasn't sure if she trusted me. Now I knew she did.

"Of course. In fact, what are you doing tonight?"

"Do you think it's sad that we're out with each other on a date night?" I sat across from Trinity in the local Greek place, the remnants of shared baklava between us.

Trinity drank from the pretty mug of Greek coffee. I'd

opted for herbal tea.

"I think it's sadder to be home alone. Unless that's what you want to do."

"I agree." I sat back against the booth bench. "I miss the girls like crazy, but I am getting to appreciate my alone time."

"Aren't they coming back for Thanksgiving next week?"

"Yes, on Wednesday." My heart dropped. "I can't stand that we haven't figure out who killed Frannie. I don't want all of this hanging over the girls' visit." I meant it. Yes, the store opening had the awful cloud of violent crime stuck over it, too. But most important to me was my girls' well-being.

"How much have you told them?"

"I had to tell them everything. You know they would have found out, if not through the grapevine known as my family, through the news."

"Maybe not. They're in different cities, and this barely made the local news."

"Only because you and your officers have done such a good job of keeping it out of the press. It must be hard to do that."

"It can be, but the local news knows we'll cooperate fully with them, that we're totally transparent, once a case is solved. If we need the public's help in finding a criminal, we never hesitate to ask, and we use the local news outlets to do so. It's always better to have a good working relationship with the press than not."

"I give you credit. In the Navy we had a unit Public Relations officer to handle it."

"That's what they pay me for." She wiped her mouth with the blue-and-white checked napkin. "This has been fun. I have to admit that when I heard you were moving back, I wasn't certain if you'd be interested in your old friends."

"Of course I am. I thought the same, too, you know. Every time your name came up over the past twenty years I heard about how accomplished you were, the hard jobs you took that got you to this position. I'm sorry we didn't make more time to see one another. And that's on me—I'm the one who was here for such short times."

"Forget about it. Regrets are a waste of time. We were both raising kids and wrapped up in our domestic dramas." Her eyes widen. "Oh my goodness, Angel, I'm sorry. I don't mean to suggest that Tom's death was a drama. Insert foot much?" She rolled her eyes.

"No offense taken. You're absolutely right." We'd talked about ourselves, our lack of social lives, but hadn't touched on the case. I knew I couldn't let her go before I told her what I found out with Amy.

"Spit it out." She'd seen my cogs turning, maybe in how I was biting my lip?

"I spoke with Amy Radabaugh a couple of days ago." I filled her in, even up to the part where I wanted to talk to Ken again. Trinity listened, her professional demeanor back in place.

"You say you saw her at the coffee shop when you were there last Saturday?"

I nodded. "Yes. She was working."

"Okay, thank you for sharing this with me. But now leave it be. It's up to my team to follow up on what she said to you. And officially, it's all hearsay as you're not—"

"Official. I know." I looked at my spoon, the used tea bag squished on it. "Can I talk to Ken?"

Trinity sighs. "I told you, you can talk to whomever you darn well please. You're at an advantage in some ways because you're new to a lot of folks here, and hopefully they'll want to help you clear the shop's name. My team's already cleared you as a suspect. But you're not trained in police work. Don't put yourself into any compromising position."

"I'll stay safe."

"I mean don't compromise the investigation, or evidence. I know you know how to take care of yourself."

"Thanks?"

She sighs. "I don't want to have to ever issue you a ticket for impeding a police investigation. That's what happens when well-meaning civilians try to do our job."

"I hear you." I finish my coffee. "I'm okay asking questions, I'm to keep passing you any facts I gather, but if I upset a potential witness or tamper with evidence, I'm screwed."

"You're a quick study, Angel."

Chapter Twenty

O N SATURDAY THE walk to Schrock Real Estate takes me three minutes, tops, but I contemplate a year's worth of possibilities on my way. I didn't give Ken a heads-up that I'm coming in as I've learned in the Navy it's almost always better to take a suspect by surprise. I had a sailor suspected of stealing from the hangar's snack bar till when I was a junior officer, and I was assigned as the investigating officer for the case. I found the young woman alone as she cleaned up a rusting aircraft panel and was able to get the facts from her in her usual environment far more easily than if I'd called her into my office and grilled her.

I'm hoping Ken won't take my prying as a grilling.

The scent of cinnamon tickles my nose as I step into the front office and the warm air is inviting. Jenna's talking on her headset, eyes glued to a computer screen, and the Christmas tree is lit up and ready for Thanksgiving to be over.

It's only a week since Frannie passed, and it's business as usual at Schrock Real Estate.

I catch Jenna's eye and point to the back hallway, mouth

"Ken?" She holds up a single finger.

"I'm sorry, I need to put you on hold for a moment. Thank you." Jenna's eyes are no longer swollen, and the woman I met months earlier is back. "Hi Angel. Let me see if Ken's available." She taps on her keyboard and after a few seconds, looks up. "He is. But only for a few minutes. We've had a deluge of clients the past few days. Let me show you back."

"I'm good." Maybe she doesn't recall I was in here last week. The days have to be a blur, no question. But I am stymied by her claim that their business has picked up. I know a realtor's busiest seasons are spring and fall, with the holidays being the slowest. I had to wait for a number of commercial properties to go up for sale last spring, and jumped as soon as my building popped up on Zillow.

She doesn't answer as she's back on her call, motioning me toward Ken's office.

He's leaning back in his executive chair, feet on the desk. I see he's sporting dark-brown acorn print socks. At least someone's keeping the current holiday. I suppose seeing Thanksgiving and fall decorations calms me as each and every Christmas light or ornament reminds me that the shop opening is that much closer. For some reason Thanksgiving, only one day before the grand opening, is my line between *I've got it, it'll all be okay* and *holy cannoli, I only have a week left to get it all together.*

Intent on the phone, his gaze watching the blustery

weather through a large window, he doesn't notice me until I give the doorjamb a little knuckle rap.

He startles, swings to face me. His expression relaxes into a grin, and he makes the circular hand gesture that signals me to come in. But not before I see the stark terror that's in his eyes.

Who was he expecting?

"I'll talk to you after the holidays, then. Okay, great." He ends his call and shakes his head. "I'll tell you, people want more and more as the years go by."

"Hi Ken."

"Uh, oh, Hi, Angel." He runs his fingers through his hair. "I haven't thanked you for the soup yet. It fed me and William the first few nights he was home." I'd dropped off a large container of navy bean soup, along with a fresh whole grain baguette, a few days ago.

"I'm glad. Is he here through the holidays?"

"Yes, through next Sunday, then he has to report back. He's already been granted Christmas leave, and we'll have the celebration of life for Frannie then."

"Who's handling it?"

"Bruckmeier and Brothers, here in town. She's... she's already been cremated."

I knew the coroner had released the body, but this makes it so real, so final. I'm merely the one who discovered her body. I can't imagine how Ken's feeling.

Forget the empathy, get the facts.

"So, Ken, I dropped in to see how you're doing. You're back to work already. Jenna told me you're busy. Is that smart? All of this has been such a shock."

"Work is my kind of therapy, Angel. I can't sit home and see the constant reminders of her."

Hmmm, fair enough.

"I know you get me, since you lost Tom the way you did. You've been here."

"In many ways, yes." But Tom's death was a long time coming. Still awful, senseless and incomprehensible, but sadly expected. Not the jarring event of Frannie's demise.

"I'm fine, Angel, really. I appreciate your concern but you don't have to check in on me."

"It's what friends do, Ken. I'm sorry we've lost touch over the years. When I spoke to Frannie that morning I had every intention of getting to see more of both of you."

He nods. "I know. She texted me the same. It was our last text." His face is solid granite, no emotion but regret in his slight frown. "Despite what the rest of town thinks, Frannie and I were close."

"Oh."

He shoots me a knowing glance. "Come off it, Angel. I know what everyone's saying. They think I did it."

"I haven't heard that, Ken." I do know that he had an alibi, though. So it couldn't have been him.

"I'm surprised. If you want to do me a favor, maybe tell your old school buddy Trinity that I'm innocent."

"Has Trinity given you any indication that she thinks you're responsible?"

"No. And she knows my alibi is solid. I was showing a house. But the good ol' Stonebridge gossip mill can't resist this kind of grist."

"What do you mean about the town gossip specifically, Ken? Please tell me to stop if I'm pushing personal boundaries here."

He shakes his head and I go on.

"I've heard that you and Frannie had a rough go of it a few years ago, sure, but I thought you'd patched things up."

He nods. "We did. I, ah, strayed from our relationship several years ago. It was the worst mistake of my life."

"I'm sorry, Ken. Tom and I had a happy marriage, but still, there are always tough times in any long-term relationship. It's called life." I hope this sounds like I understand. Which for the most part is true except it's really difficult for me to understand anyone stepping out on their spouse when it's far simpler to admit the love has died and move on. Or better, talk about problems before they become life altering.

Ken slams his fist on the desk. "I made a real effin'—sorry, Angel—mess of it."

"Please, don't even think about it. I was in the Navy." I know swear phrases that make Ken's words sound like a nursery rhyme. "How did Frannie find out that you'd strayed?"

"That's the worst part. I was involved with one of our

assistants."

"Jenna?" Shock straightens my spine. The assistant who put up with Frannie's less-than-kind bossiness?

"No, no, never Jenna. God no. It was someone who's left the office. Liza. She had to go, once Frannie found out. Frannie, uh, found out about us, what we were doing." He doesn't meet my gaze. "In the break room. But she wasn't the one to see us...I still don't know who did." He offers a hollow laugh. "Nothing escaped Frannie. I swear she had eyes all over this town."

"I'm so sorry, Ken." I hope he's done sharing. I really don't need all of these details. So far, Ken's being true to what I've put together from Crystal and Trinity. Disappointment wells. I'm not getting any closer to helping Trinity close this case.

"I was the epitome of the guy who had it all, and almost lost it all." Ken appears prepared to bare his soul. I can't rush out after pumping him so blatantly for information that really is none of my business. Except for the Frannie being murdered in my shop part.

"That's in the past, Ken. I'm sure Frannie knew how much you love her." I cross my fingers under my long scarf. Frannie's words about Ken weren't so kind that morning in front of Latte Love, but Ken doesn't need that information.

"Fortunately Frannie forgave me and we were able to make a go of it again. I went to counseling for several months, of course. And we did marriage therapy together.

Plus, Eloise had this couples sexuality yoga class that was a lot of fun."

I nod, try to appear encouraging. I can't help but wonder about his and Frannie's former assistant, Liza. What help had she received, after a person in authority over her became sexually involved with her? I want to keep Ken comfortable, though, so I keep this observation to myself. And make a mental note to ask Crystal if she knows more about Liza.

I can't think of someone who'd have a better motive to kill Frannie than Ken's ex-lover.

"How long ago was this?"

"Earlier this year."

Wait. This is completely different from the timeline Crystal described. Had Ken had more than one affair? And he didn't seem to know about Max. As in, Frannie and Max. Ugh. I can't take Ken totally off the suspect list but if he thought they were reconciled and had zero knowledge of Frannie's fling with Max, why would he want Frannie dead?

I need to find Liza.

THE REST OF the day is filled with the finishing touches on the construction. Phil and the team agreed to work through the weekend, much to my relief. Phil promises tomorrow is the last day Max and the team will need to show up before the sun does. It'll give me a few days to perfect the displays, pick the best spots to set up the folding tables with holiday beverages and treats.

I slip out for Saturday Mass, but only because I know Phil will be there when I return. I can't stomach the thought of coming back into an empty shop like last Saturday. When it was anything but empty.

"That's just about it, Angel. A couple of these guys will be back in the morning to do a thorough clean sweep, but other than that, we're done."

"I owe you, Phil. I realize you don't usually work weekends."

"Don't mention it. It's the least I could do. One thing you'll find out is that when the you-know-what hits the fan, Stonebridge comes together. Doesn't matter who you vote for, which side of any issue you're on. When it comes down to it, we're a tight-knit community."

"I'm discovering that, actually. I can't get over how much support everyone is showing me." After I showed up at the Buddies meeting and made it clear that I wasn't going to stop until I found the murderer.

Phil nods. "You keep your chin up. The police'll wrap this up and it'll be a sad chapter, but a closed one."

"Thanks, Phil."

Alone again I get back to my to-do list, which has exponentially grown each day. So many items need to wait until the day before or day of the opening, next Saturday.

MY FOLKS SURPRISE me with my favorite restaurant food, takeout, just as I'm about to take Ralph and me upstairs for the night. Since Frannie's murder, I'm loathe to spend time alone in my office after nightfall.

"Honey, your father and I are here to help. No arguments, please." Mom and Dad sit at my kitchen table, the remains of our Greek takeout strewn in front of us. I'm taking the last sip of my water, gathering the energy to clear the table.

"Your mother's right, Angel. You've got the girls coming in, Thanksgiving, and the shop opening."

"And a murder in your shop." Mom shivers and Dad widens his eyes at her. "Well, it's true. No use denying what happened."

"The funeral's tomorrow." I know it's cliché and the result of my favorite streaming documentaries, but Stonebridge is a small place. The chances of Frannie's murderer being at the ceremony aren't tiny.

"Her poor family. I don't know what Marcie's going to do without her. Frannie was the sun and moon to her and Fred."

My gut tightens and I blink. When Tom died, I thought I'd used up my tear production quota. Until I lost a friend and colleague in combat. Then the girls left for college. The emotions swirling in my heart feel too close to self-pity, so I side step them. Sure, I'm disappointed that the life change I'm making isn't going to be able to be as exuberant, but at least I'm still here. As in on planet Earth. Frannie doesn't have the option.

"Now, Livvie, you can't fix everything."

"I know Douglas, I know."

My parents' dialogue is as familiar and worn as a favorite pair of slippers. It's exactly the comfort I need. I gather the empty containers I go to the sink and rinse them.

"You know, honey, I can't stop thinking about how Frannie's loss is so much bigger than anyone realizes. Take my eel weir project. She was a voice that I'm afraid I can't replace."

"What do you mean, Mom?" I remember that Crystal told me Frannie was certain the weir is authentic, ancient, but Frannie's motives were different from my Mom's and most historians, I'd think. Mom wants history preserved, learned from. Frannie wanted to put Stonebridge on the lifestyles of the uber-rich map.

"Frannie didn't just have connections, she had pull with just about all of them." Judging from the gleam in her eye, Mom's about to wax on over the weir. I glance at Dad, who's quietly listening.

"Hang on Mom, I want to ask you more questions. Anyone want decaf coffee?"

All three of us do, so I put a pot on.

"Shouldn't we be taking this downstairs with us? We're

here to help with the store inventory." Mom's back to running my business. Trying to, anyhow.

"Mom, I'm good. And I'm not going back in the shop tonight. What did you always say before one of us had an exam the next day, Dad?"

"That a good night's sleep will set anything right again."

"Exactly." I pull half-and-half from the refrigerator and frozen green beans from the freezer. Ralph gets a bowl of warm veggies each night. "I'm going to enjoy my time with you and Ralph without worrying about the shop. Besides, I'm just about ready."

I'm lying. There's a lot more work to be done. But my mind is otherwise engaged. Figuring out who killed Frannie.

We head into the living room, and I pop on the gas-insert fireplace. It was one of the modern concessions I made, but it's inside the original fireplace, with the marble mantel intact.

"This is so cozy. You've done a wonderful job in here, Angel." Mom takes the large easy chair and plops her stockinged feet on my blue damask ottoman. Dad takes the sofa, leaning on an overstuffed Belgian tapestry throw pillow that features—what else?—a Santa holding a parrot. It was a spectacular find in Ghent, when I took the girls for weekend afternoons away from the NATO base.

I sit cross-legged on the handwoven silk rug from Turkey, my back to the fire, facing my parents. We're all holding oversized mugs of varying designs. I still haven't gotten around to switching in my holiday mugs, though. That's for after Thanksgiving, and a task I'll delegate to Ava and Lily, who both enjoy decorating.

"Your store and parts of the house are ready for Christmas."

"I usually don't like doing any Christmas decorations before Thanksgiving. But this year I had to start early, for the store's sake, don't you think?"

"For this year, sure. Your father hates that they put out Christmas before Halloween these days." Mom's code for *I hate it.*

"I hear you, Mom." I lean in. "Mom, what were you saying about the weir and Frannie?"

Mom's eyes narrow. "I think I've expressed my opinion. Why don't you tell me what you're looking for, honey?"

I laugh. There's no pulling anything over on Mom.

"Bam! Right in the kisser." Dad's exuberance makes all three of us laugh.

"I'm wondering if Frannie's push to make the weir a big tourist attraction angered the wrong person."

Mom blinks. Dad sucks in a breath.

"Honey, don't tell me you think anyone in the historical society is capable of murder?" Mom frowns, then rolls her eyes. "We all love history and Stonebridge is rich with it. But not enough to commit a crime over!"

"What about when you staked out the meeting house against the wishes of the police, Livvie?" Dad's face is expressionless but his eyes glimmer with repressed glee. He loves teasing Mom about her sometimes over-the-top methods.

"That wasn't illegal, per se, Douglas, and you know it. How else were we going to catch the graffiti artist?"

"But you didn't catch him or her. And you crushed Marilyn Carver's prized rose bushes. She was expected to win first place, you know."

Mom says some words that rival the saltiest sailors I ever knew. "You're just stirring the pot, Douglas."

Dad is, but it's the best entertainment going in front of my fire tonight.

"Honey, you should go talk to Mel if you're interested in the weir. And especially Frannie's involvement in promoting it. He might be able to give you more information than me." But her tone reflects her doubt.

"Mel? The same Mel who's always run it?" The man I'm thinking of can't possibly be alive. He was ancient when I grew up here.

"Same man, yes. He's nearing ninety-five, I think. But he doesn't look a day over ninety, truly."

Mom's eyes are guarded, so I do what all good daughters do. I press her. "You really don't think Frannie's pressure on the town was enough to send the wrong person over the mental cliff and harm her?"

Mom's mouth twists, puckers, rests in a straight line. "I think a lot of people would have preferred she stay out of it, at least until we confirm it's thousands of years old. We tried to explain to her that even if it's only a colonial rip-off of the Native originals, it has its place in Stonebridge history and the story, all of it, needs to be told. But you know Frannie..." Mom sips her coffee. "Or rather, knew her."

"How so, Mom?"

"I think your mother's trying to say that Frannie only saw what she wanted to see, and expected others to fall in line, no question." Dad doesn't usually speak for Mom like this so I know this must have been a topic of conversation between them. As in, Frannie annoyed the heck out of Mom.

"Is Dad right, Mom?"

"Pretty much, yes."

We sit in companionable silence for several minutes and I soak it all up. It might the quietest moments I'll have in a long while. It's certainly the most relaxed I've felt since last Saturday afternoon.

"Tell you what, guys. I'll take you up on your offers."

"Which one, Angel?" Mom sounds like she's holding her breath. Dad's quiet, watching me with his steady gaze.

"Both. Dad, you can go pick up Ava in Pittsburgh on Wednesday. Mom, you can take the train, same day, to get Lily." Lily, at Temple, was an easy two-hour train ride away. "I'll switch my ticket to your name."

"Wonderful! You know I love the train. I can knit the whole time." Mom's been working on secret Christmas projects but we all suspect we're getting matching ski caps.

Last year she made us scarves, with our names duplicate-stitched over the premium cashmere blend yarn that Bryce claimed was "one of a kind" from a "small quantities producer."

"Maybe you shouldn't take anything that will distract you, dear. You have to get off at the station in Philly to change trains." Dad can't help from making sure Mom's enthusiasm doesn't steer her off course, even almost a week out.

"Do I have to remind you who the Temple alumna is?" Mom's eyes sparkle. She pushes back the ottoman, stands up, leans over the sofa to plant a big one on Dad's mouth. Dad blushes and I get up on my feet.

My quiet interlude is kaput.

I've got another person to interview first thing tomorrow. Luckily for me, the historical society is open especially for the holidays and I can make a quick jaunt there in between stocking my shelves. Will Mel be the one that leads me to Frannie's murderer?

Chapter Twenty-One

"*WOOF! Ooowwww!*"

Ralph flutters his wings in disapproval as the canine sounds wake him from his Sunday morning parrot slumber atop the cage in my office. I wheeled him in here with me when we came down right after breakfast.

"*Eeeetch.*" His half-hearted complaint makes me giggle.

"I feel the same way, buddy." No energy left to spend on being afraid, or shocked, by Frannie's murder. It's time to solve it. Right after I get some more work done.

"*Eeeetch!*" More forcefully as the dog noises sound closer.

Ralph's never going to let his new exclamation go, I'm afraid. Whenever something disturbs him, he's screeched his new mystery word. Which computes to dozens of times this past week.

"It's okay, Ralph. Someone's just walking their dog."

"Woof." Steps scrambling on the back stoop raise goose-bumps on my flesh. But before I can tell myself or Ralph to calm down, there's a knock at the back door.

I freeze. I'm certain the killer came in through the back door, and being alone as I am, save for Ralph, I can't help my mind's flashbacks. Suddenly my inviting storage room is again a grisly murder scene, the broken Santa lodged—

"*Oooowww!*" More knocking, lots more footfalls. More like paw-falls.

The security system.

Frantic, I look for the tablet, posed on its easel next to the coffee pot. I zero in on the lower right corner, where a tall man fills the lens.

Nate.

My heart trips into pounding of a different kind. This kind of surprise, I can handle. I get my keys, tell Ralph to relax as I quickly put him inside his cage, and open the back door.

A blast of November wind blows in dried ginseng leaves and the scent of…Nate. Roasted coffee beans, caramel, and a clean piney aroma.

"Nate! Hi, Mach!"

"Hey, we're sorry to bother you but, ah, I heard you were in the shop today and I wanted to talk to you."

"Sure. Come on in."

Mach bounds ahead of Nate, and Nate tugs him back with the Eagles leash. Same Phillies collar, too.

"You need a holiday-themed leash and collar set, Mach." I grin at Nate. "We have quite the assortment of everything from traditional holiday plaid, to blue-and-white with silver dreidels, to snowflakes."

"Mach's more of a sports dude." Nate takes his ski cap

off, revealing that crop of startling silver hair.

"Woof!" Mach's not interested in anything but Ralph, who has his beak up against his cage wires.

"Pretty bird. Give me a kiss!" Ralph's acting more himself than he has all week. Except it seems to be enticing Mach.

"I wouldn't let him get too close to the cage—"

Mach lets out a pitiful yelp as he bounces backward from the cage, his tail swinging in all directions.

"Mach, calm down, boy. Stop. No, Mach, no!"

"Oh no!"

Nate and I yell in unison as Mach's wide, fluffy, very long tail makes a clean sweep of the table next to my desk. The neat pile of felted nativity figures I was prepping to put out in the shop scatter in a burst of bright colors. Soft *thuds* sound as a camel, sheep, donkey, Mary, Joseph and two of the three Magi hit the floor.

"Mach! Sit." Mach's butt makes an audible plop and his tail thumps in what I can only describe as happiness, his intelligent gaze meeting Nate's briefly before he turns his attention back to Ralph.

"Eyes on me, Mach." Nate's frustration is evident in his tone, but to be fair, none of this is the dog's fault. Or Nate's. It just is. I notice a telltale red spot on Mach's nose.

"Ralph, you are in so much trouble." I kneel down in front of Mach, who is thrilled with the attention and promptly licks my entire face. "Poor boy. I'm so sorry, Nate, but Ralph bit him on the snout."

Nate looks, shakes his head. "He's fine. Maybe it'll teach him to leave Ralph alone."

"Doubtful. Ralph's a master seducer." As soon as the words are out I feel the heat in my cheeks. I cough. "I mean, he's done this to almost every dog he's met. My sister's labs have had their share of nips since we moved back."

"I'm going to reimburse you for the damaged goods." Nate's looking around, and I follow his gaze. The nativity figures are spread over the floor, between my desk and the coffee counter.

"No reimbursement necessary. It's okay." I bend down and pick up a couple Magi. "Look, they're all made of felt, so nothing broken."

"Mach needs to learn to behave better. He's already two."

"He's still a young pup, right Mach?" Mach lets me scratch behind his ears. "Let me get him some peroxide for his nose." I've picked up most of the figures, but as I count I notice I'm still missing one.

"That's not necessary." Nate's face is flushed, too. The rosy glow brings out his eyes, the cut of his jaw. I turn my attention back to searching for the missing nativity figure, recount what I've picked up.

"Huh."

"What's missing?" Nate's brows draw together.

"Nothing, please." But I can't help my gaze from bouncing around the edges of the room, where the hardwood floor meets the wall. Mach's tail keeps thumping.

"Let me help look." He sets the leash down and walks over. "What is it we're searching for?"

"Baby Jesus. He's tiny, about the size of my thumb, with a pale blue blanket."

"Okay."

We bend down at the same time and immediately bonk heads.

"Ow!" I'm not seeing stars, exactly. More like a meteor shower.

"Oof." Nate rubs his forehead. "This is so not going the way I'd planned."

"What are you talking about?"

"I suppose this is the worst time to ask you out."

"Out?"

"You know, on a date."

NATE'S QUESTION AND my gut-reaction answer—I agreed to let him take me to dinner tomorrow night—has my head spinning so fast that I almost forget the most important thing I have planned for the day. I swear, if I hadn't set the alert on my phone calendar I would have sat in my office for hours after Nate and Mach left. Staring into space, letting myself enjoy the afterglow of realizing my attraction to Nate isn't one-sided.

But work and solving Frannie's murder prevail. I just spent the last hour learning more than I thought possible about my hometown.

"Thanks for agreeing to show me around, Mel. I really appreciate it." Melvin Springer stands in front of the Historical Society's wall-sized map of Stonebridge, circa 1878. The town was founded nearly a century before and the area settled almost two hundred years ago. I keep looking at the scant inch between Mel's bald head and the ceiling of the log cabin home where the society is headquartered. It's a miracle he hasn't cracked his noggin on one of the lower-hanging exposed beams.

"It's what I do." He looks around the room, from the glass cases that hold various artifacts both Native and colonial, to the shelf of antique books that offer a glimpse into the merchants who shaped Stonebridge. Most notable is Jacob Stoner, the namesake for Jacob's Run, the home of the eel weir. Which is what I'm really here to find out about.

"Did you happen to know Frannie Schrock very well, Mel?"

He nods, blinks behind rimless specs. "I saw her parents grow up. My family lived down the road from their farm. Awful what happened to her. In your shop, no less." His gaze is steady, nonjudgmental.

"Yes. I've heard it mentioned that Frannie was sold on the eel weir being authentically Native. Do you know why?"

"Look here." He points to the map, to where Jacob's Run is located north of town and runs parallel with Main Street for almost a mile before making several S turns and flowing east where it eventually meets the Susquehanna. His arthritic hand moves across the Plexiglas that protects the old paper until his finger stops on a point west of town.

"Woodsman's Grove?" I'm familiar with the area that's been set aside as game lands.

"Uh huh. There's more than one eel weir, but Frannie focused on the one here." He points to a spot almost dead center above Stonebridge. Almost directly north of my building. "For good reason, as it's close to town and officially a part of Stonebridge, just like Jacob's Run."

"But that doesn't explain why it's authentic, original. As in, thousands instead of hundreds of years old."

Mel holds up his index finger, makes sure he has my attention. "It does, though. The older ruins are all under water back here, and here." He indicates locations before Stonebridge proper begins. "And over here, we know that the weirs are no more than a few hundred years old. That's been proven."

"Past town. So the one here in Stonebridge could be somewhere in between?"

He shakes his head. Mel's made up his mind, it seems. "No, not in between. Our weir is definitely Native, and may even be the oldest one ever found. I don't need to wait for the college researchers to get their results in. They found a bevy of arrowheads and other items in the same exact location. All of those predated the other Native weirs. So it's fair to say these rocks are original. Have you ever been to Rome in your Navy travels? Italy?"

"Yes."

"Okay, great. So you've seen how they incorporate ancient ruins into contemporary settings."

"As a matter of fact, there are ruins in the Navy Exchange in Napoli, Italy. You can see them through the floor."

"And in the UK, there are many examples of ruins coexisting with modern architecture."

"But the eel weir is underwater. How will it drive more visitors to Stonebridge?" I'm still not seeing why Frannie was so hot about the weir.

"The Historical Society already has plans drawn up for a visitor's center adjacent Jacob's Run."

"Do you mean like the one in Gettysburg? On Stonebridge town property?" The thought of the bucolic fields and trees surrounding Jacob's Run being paved for an edifice of any kind leaves me cold.

"Yes. But without Frannie's support, I'm afraid it'll never pass."

"Why would you think that? It's going to be a matter of scientific fact, right?" Either the weir is ancient, or it isn't.

"No, that's just it. Like your mother and most of the society, I hope to heck that this is an ancient structure. In my gut, I believe it is. But let's say it isn't, that it's only a couple hundred years old."

"That's still historical."

"Yes. But not historical enough to warrant the visitor's center, and resulting PR money to run ads to entice tourists. Frannie wasn't going to rest until Stonebridge was featured in every Pennsylvania tourism video spot, be it on television, social media, or the town's website. She had the pull to make it all happen, and it was close, let me tell you. But now..." He shakes his head, the sun reflecting off the very top more than at his temples.

I mentally kick myself for judging Mel's lack of hair, of all things. What is my problem?

You're stressed and under the gun about the opening.

Maybe.

"Are you saying that Frannie was going to get the approval for the building project pushed through before the actual age was identified?"

"You got it." Mel's eyes are sharp, belying the age spots on his head. "She wanted it passed before we knew, in fact. So that even if the weir's ten years old, some kind of high school prank, the budget for the building structure would already be passed. She figured the worst thing that would happen is the building's purpose would be redefined. Either way, it's a Stonebridge town building, available for one and all to use for their annual events. She was already talking about a possible folk fest. Can you imagine? Emmy Lou

Harris or Dolly Parton, here in Stonebridge."

"That's impressive. You might be able to get my favorite, Brandi Carlile, in here." I've become a huge Americana music fan since returning to the States.

"Is she related to the Carlisles of Carlisle?" Mel's referring to the larger town to the west and south of Stonebridge. For the record, I don't expect Mel to know who Brandi Carlile is, but come on. If you're going to talk folk music, there's no one better than Brandi and the Hanseroth twins.

"No, no relation."

"Well, you can invite whomever you want if we ever get it built. I just doubt that it's going to happen, to be honest."

"Mel, is there any member of the Historical Society, or anyone you can think of, that would be hurt if the Stonebridge Center is built? Financially or otherwise?"

The vacant look in his eyes frightens me. *Please don't stroke out now. Please.*

"As it turns out, I'm a permanent member of the town's development advisory board. I know what you're getting at, Livvie." I don't correct him. If he thinks I'm my mother, that's fine by me. "I suppose whoever owns the surrounding property that needed to be purchased to make the parking lot, with room for concessions. A small music arena has been discussed, too."

"Exactly! That's who I need to talk to. Any ideas?"

He lets out a low whistle, laughs. "Oh, boy. That reminds me. You may want to take notes." He waves his hand toward my phone, where I've been tapping in pertinent facts. Mel's really good at drawing things out and while I appreciate the skill when being told about history, my jaw is clenching as the last of my patience ekes out.

"I'm ready when you are, Mel."

"Cornelia Applebaum has been mighty ticked off by all of Frannie's shenanigans."

"Is she part of the family that owns Applebaum farm?" I frequent their quaint but fully modern farmers market on a weekly basis. They're open year-round, but with fewer veggies and more locally processed dairy during the winter months.

"It's still hers, yes, but her kids have been running it for years now. Cornelia tells them where to keep it like it's always been, and they do all the technology business."

"So you were saying, Frannie angered Mrs. Applebaum?"

"Oh, more than angered. She got herself worked up enough to get a lawyer, who got her even angrier when Cornelia heard the words *eminent domain*."

"That only applies to land that the government needs use of, not private interests."

Mel stares at me, the keen intelligence in his gaze unmistakable. "That's just it, Angel." So he does know my name. "Frannie had some hotshot lawyer draw up papers stating that the museum and surrounding buildings were essential to the preservation of Stonebridge's heritage and legacy. Now, I don't know all the legalese, mind you, but I know enough.

It'd crank me up, too, if that happened to me."

"You've been so much help, Mel. I'm sorry if I came in here with my nose up in the air." Truly, I'd missed judged the nonagenarian. "I'm out of my depth."

Mel nods. "You are." My stomach clenches at his stern expression. Self-recrimination floods my face with embarrassed heat.

"I won't do it again."

"Ha!" The grave wrinkles transform into laugh lines as Mel has a solid chuckle. He taps my upper arm. "I'm just joshing you! You should have seen your face!"

It takes me a few heartbeats before I join in on Mel's mirth. Nothing like having my ego smashed right after Nate's surprise invitation bolstered it. I guess this is what's referred to as balance.

"You caught me. Thank you again so much."

"Just make sure you're keeping your police friend in the loop on all of this." Mel takes a pipe from his jacket and puts it between yellowed but very strong teeth.

Not only has he missed absolutely nothing, he's totally on to my motives.

I pray the killer isn't.

Chapter Twenty-Two

"THANKS FOR MEETING me, Sis. I do realize this is one of your busiest weeks of the year." Monday morning Crystal and I are ensconced in a back booth at Latte Love, our coffee cooling on the polished walnut table. We both grabbed a drip—Honduran for me and a proprietary holiday blend for Crystal—as we don't have time to wait on specialty coffee today.

"I figured it had to be important to you. So shoot." Crystal leans in.

"I've narrowed my suspect list down to two with the most potential."

"Go on."

"I went and saw Mel, you know, Historical Society Mel, yesterday."

"Okay."

"Mom gave me the idea. And Mel gave me lots of ideas." I rehash all I learned yesterday afternoon, watching Crystal's reaction for any sense of disbelief or bewilderment. I've never worked on a murder case before and I know the possibility of my snooping going off the rails is not only real, but probable.

Before I'm through, Crystal holds up her hand, palm-out. I notice there's not one finger without a bandage and guilt over taking her from her workbench yanks on my focus. "Let me think a minute, Angel. Your main idea is that someone working on the weir issue, someone like Mom, killed Frannie?"

"Hang on. Let me finish." I take a sip of coffee and give myself a few seconds to appreciate the rich, dark blend. "Yes, at first I thought that it would be that straightforward. Figure out who's most upset about Frannie pushing the Stonebridge Museum and building complex forward regardless of historical authenticity. But that would eliminate no one, and leave all fifty-five members of the historical society."

"Maybe they all went in on a contract?"

"Very funny. This is Pennsylvania, not New Jersey." I remind Crystal that it's not her favorite binge-watch, *The Sopranos.*

"We don't know that, Angel." Her face remains frozen in her deadpan way that tells me she's kidding.

"Accepting that the entire group can't be to blame, and there are no singular standouts—you know, folks who had public or known altercations with Frannie—that takes me back to ground zero."

"Except?" Crystal knows me well.

"Except, there's a problem with Frannie's plan. Stone-bridge owns the property surrounding Jacob's Run, on either side. Allowing for seasonal flooding—which is getting worse each year—there's zero room left for parking lots, a café or two, a gift shop. You get my drift, right?"

"I do. What or who backs up to that land?" She stares off to the left, and I can all but see her mental cogs grinding. Crystal slaps the table and grins. "The Applebaum farm!"

"Exactly!"

We laugh and high-five, our private way of sharing excitement. Okay, not so private as we're in Latte Love and as I look around, several pairs of eyes are on us.

"Sorry, folks." I offer an apologetic smile and look at Crystal, who's giggling behind her hand.

"You don't have to apologize. How many phones have rung since we sat down?"

"Hey, you're a long-time member of the Stonebridge citizens' network. The jury's still out on me, and some probably still think I had something to do with the murder."

"Can you blame them, Angel? You didn't but you've made it your project. Please tell me you understand that the minute you finish interrogating anyone in town, they spread it all over."

"I'm not interrogating anyone. It's called investigating."

"Except you're not in an official role. Are you sure Trinity's okay with all of this?"

"She's not thrilled but understands I'm going to do what I'm going to do. And I promised to tell her everything and anything I find out, of course."

"Make sure you do. So is Cornelia Applebaum your next subject?"

"Cornelia, and of course Liza Wiegela. I haven't found out where Liza lives, though."

"That won't be hard."

"What do you mean?"

Crystal freezes, stares at me. "You're kidding. You, Stonebridge's Reluctant Agatha Christie, don't know something?"

"Knock it off, Sis. If I knew half as much as you do about the local population, I'd have already solved this."

"Touchy, touchy." Crystal eyes me before patting my hand. "I'm sorry. You are super stressed and I'm teasing you." I'm not fooled by my sister's compassionate turn, not with the way the side of her mouth is twitching. She's dying to tell me something and can't wait to see my reaction.

"Spit it out, Crystal."

"The thing is, you only have one more trip to make if you think either of these women are your killer, or know of the murderer."

"Because?" If I thought I wanted to make Mel speak faster, I was mistaken. My fingers are itching to pry Crystal's mouth open and get her words out.

"Liza Wiegela is Cornelia's granddaughter."

"Wait—what? Liza is an Applebaum?"

"Yes, but she wasn't raised here—her father settled in Pittsburgh. She grew up in there, moved here for college, and worked on the farm and at the Applebaum Market through college. She studied real estate and interned at Frannie and Ken's. That's how she got hired. But once she worked there, she never pursued getting her license. She got distracted, I'd say."

"That's a nice way to say *involved with Ken*. How old is she, by the way?"

"I don't know, maybe fifteen, twenty years younger than you?"

"No wonder Frannie was furious." Betrayal is ugly no matter what, but to be traded in for someone young enough to be your daughter, ouch.

"Oh, yeah. Like I've said before, it was an awful time for Frannie and Ken."

"I'd wondered if Liza had left town." I'd made a note to ask Jenna, or better, Trinity, the next time I spoke to her.

"I think she did leave for a bit. And I have no idea if she's working for the farm again. But you can ask Cornelia all of that. She'll definitely know where Liza is, I'm guessing."

"I'll be you're right." Finally, the pieces weren't completely all over the place. I have two people to focus on, and either one could lead to the break I've been hoping for.

"Hey, Angel." Nate's standing in front of our table and I can't help but smile back at his warm greeting.

"Hi! Working on the books?" I didn't see him at the counter when I came in, and it would have been too weird to ask for him. Not until we have this first date and see where it will go. Not that I'm expecting it to go anywhere, of course. But if it did…

"Always." His gaze never leaves mine.

"Morning, Nate. I'm enjoying the holiday blend. Is nutmeg your secret?" Crystal's way of clearing her throat to interrupt the mutual admiration society.

"That's part of it. There's some elf dust in there, too." He slowly turns to my sister as if he'd rather keep looking at me. I'm not certain what to do with my observation.

Why not just enjoy it?

I can't relax and lean into anything, even the prep for opening Shop 'Round the World. Not while Frannie's murder is unsolved. I owe it to her. To anyone who'd have been murdered in my building, frankly.

"Whatever it is, it's delicious."

"Thank you. I'm glad." He flashes another smile at us both. "I'm off, just wanted to say hi. See you later." He taps the table in front of my mug before walking away.

Once he's definitely out of earshot, Crystal nudges me with her shoulder.

"Dish. What's *later* all about?"

I could prevaricate, keep her guessing. But I'm thinking that in that Stonebridge's grapevine-is-faster-than-the-speed-of-sound way, Crystal might already know.

"It's a date. Nothing more, nothing less."

Chapter Twenty-Three

THE DRIVE OUT to the Applebaum's on Monday afternoon doesn't take me more than ten minutes. I checked with my mom to see if Cornelia still lives in the original farmhouse and I'm glad I did. Turns out Cornelia turned the homestead over to one of her son's and had her own house built half a mile away on the same farm property. Chickens run across the graveled drive as I pull in front of the Craftsman style house, which looks more like a beachside cottage.

I'm greeted by no less than three cats as I climb the wide porch steps, admiring the simple yet effective autumnal decor. Three large pumpkins, one a traditional squash, one white, and the other a Cinderella pumpkin—which is really a gourd that makes delicious soup—are arranged about a bale of hay. An oak leaf garland hangs over the doorframe, with matching wreath on the gray painted door. I press the doorbell and stand a bit back, so that I'm in view of the security camera. I want to make sure Cornelia doesn't think I'm a solicitor or other unwanted visitor.

The door opens wide without warning and a tall, distinguished woman with cream cookie hair grins at me.

"Is that you, Angel Warren?"

"Yes, ma'am. How are you?"

"I'm good, thank you, but wondering what on earth brings you out here on such a blustery day. You've got a shop to get opened, don't you?"

"I do, but I need to ask you some questions if you have a few minutes."

"You caught me in between my Bible study and golf." She stands back and ushers me in. "Go ahead and sit down. Would you like something to drink? And I've got fresh pumpkin pie from the store. I don't bake myself any longer, why bother when they use my recipes?" Her laugh tinkles through the living room, where I sit on a well-worn and very comfortable blue gingham sofa.

"Oh no, I'm not here to be entertained. As much as I love Applebaum's bakery. You know I've ordered several items for the grand opening from here."

"Oh, have you? That's wonderful." She sits across from me. "I'm not involved in the business at all these days, but I do like to hear when a customer is happy."

I don't believe her for one nanosecond. According to my mother, Cornelia is the rock of Applebaum's Market to this day. She may not run the numbers or place orders, but she is the creative muse that makes it a success.

"You're being too modest, but we can argue that another time. I'm here because of what happened in my shop last week."

"The murder." She nods. "My study group was buzzing about it. I find it hard to believe they haven't caught the murderer yet. Stonebridge isn't a big town. Of course, it could have been a random break-in, I suppose."

Whoa. "I see you've given this a lot of thought, then?"

"It's hard not to, when my Liza went through all that she did with those two." She smooths her blue jeans over slim thighs. "I'm just grateful Liza quit before she ruined her life. She's moved on to better things, for certain."

"Oh?" I want to know everything about Liza, but first things first. The Stonebridge Museum. "I'm glad to hear that. I'm here to clarify what exactly was going on with the plans to build the Stonebridge Museum. Specifically, on your property."

"I'll tell you where it's going—nowhere." Exasperation twists her mouth. "I'm not against bringing more people into town. The more tourists, the merrier! But Frannie was barking up the wrong tree on that one. We haven't established if the eel weir is ancient or not, and even if it is, it'd take years to come up with an effective way to highlight it. It is underwater, after all."

"I heard that the town was going to try to take some of your property alongside Jacob's Run for the project?"

"That was Frannie's hope, but according to my lawyers, it's moot. There are plenty of other locations around Jacob's creek that can be used, the vast majority of acreage belonging to the state."

"Stone Cliff State Park." Of course! I'd overlooked it because it shares its boundary with an adjacent town.

Cornelia nods. "Yes. What's better? Because the park runs across the back of Silver Maple's border, the project can be a joint one. Two towns bring more to the money pot than one."

"That makes total sense. To be honest, I feel a little stupid that I didn't think of that."

"You just moved back, and you have a business to run. Why would this abstract plan of Frannie's be in your sights? Except of course, with her murder in your building, it's your primary concern."

"It is. I appreciate your understanding, Mrs. Applebaum."

She waves at me as if batting a gnat. "Please. Call me Cornelia. You're not a little kid begging for a sample of candy apple any longer." She refers to the confection of the season's crispest apples dipped in a clear red syrup that hardens into a candy shell.

"I used to love those!" Until one dislodged a baby molar when I was eleven.

"We all did. But they're hell on a dental bridge!" We both laugh, Cornelia more robustly. I've noticed that septuagenarians and older find humor in things that still horrify my mid-life sensibilities. No one's getting younger but I'm not ready to rush into the second half of my life.

"Thank you for sharing that with me. About your property." Unbeknownst to Cornelia, she's occupied my suspect list for the shortest time of anyone. And now she's a definite cross-off.

Which leaves one significant possibility.

"Anytime, Angel. I'm so sorry that Frannie met her end the way she did, and in your store. Just awful. But if I can, I'd like to give you some advice. Take it or leave it."

I'm all ears. "Okay."

Her eyes shine with conviction behind red cat-eye frames. "Nothing good happens in that real estate office. Liza lost herself when she worked there, and took the blame for things that Frannie and her husband were responsible for. A marriage gone bad is like poison that hurts the surrounding family and friends a heck of a lot more."

"What is Liza doing these days, if you don't mind me asking?"

"We FaceTime every week. She's such a dear. Let's see, last week she was learning how to make dresses from recycled fabric. That's on top of her regular job, working with and teaching the locals how to install and maintain an irrigation system."

"Where is Liza, Cornelia?"

"Namibia, Africa. She's in the Peace Corps."

Which explains why I haven't been able to find her. No social media accounts under Liza Wiegela exist according to my recent search.

"I had no idea. Thank you for sharing that with me."

"I'm happy to. It took her longer than my other grands, to find her way. She figured out that office work isn't for her."

"I am sorry about her experience at Schrock Real Estate. Do you think she'd have time, or be willing, to talk to me?" I don't have to ascertain an alibi from her, not if she's in Africa. But I still have some unanswered questions about her time in with Ken and Frannie.

"I don't see why not. She is very busy, though."

"When is she coming home?"

"She's halfway through. In another year."

We exchange phone numbers and I invite her to my grand opening, with the promise of a stellar spread of Applebaum caramel apples, pumpkin pie, and their signature gingerbread ice cream that I plan to serve from a vintage French Champagne cooler I found at the Tongeren flea market in Belgium.

"I'll be there on Saturday, Angel, rain or shine!" Cornelia waves from the front porch as I reverse out of the drive and turn onto the road back into the center of town.

As the farm fields give way to lumbering oak trees that tower over Stonebridge's residential streets, I realize I'm most likely not going to be the one to solve Frannie's murder. I'm totally okay with this, as long as the murderer is caught, tried, and justice is served. Before I second-guess myself, I call Trinity via my hands-free phone.

"Colson."

"Hey, Trin, how are you doing?"

"Fair to stormy." We both laugh. "What's up?"

"I've found out some things I think you should know. Any chance you'll have a spare fifteen minutes today or tomorrow?"

"Is any of this urgent?"

"No, not really. I'm following up on my promise to let you know what I'm up to."

"And I appreciate that. How does tomorrow morning work?"

"Perfect. Where and when?"

"Your shop, eight o'clock?" Trinity knows I'm an early riser and am working 'round the clock right now.

"I'll have the coffee waiting."

"Bye."

We disconnect as I pull into my parking space behind the shop. I sit in the quiet under the bare limbed maple and mentally review all I've learned since Frannie died. I may not have solved the crime, but I've gotten to know Stonebridge in ways I couldn't have unless something major prodded me. I'd planned to keep to my corner of the world, love my girls whenever they were home or visited, be there for my family.

Now I know that it wasn't enough. Being present, listening, getting to know folks is what matters at the end of the day. With the engine off the inside of the car quickly chills, and I chuckle to myself as I get out and walk to my building.

I can tell myself all the sweet sentiments I want to, but the truth is that I want Frannie's murder solved in the worst way. It would be nice to have this behind me before Saturday. Heck, before Wednesday, when the girls get home.

What about before tomorrow night?

I can't add solving the murder to the pressure of my first date with Nate. It wouldn't be right. But it would be so very nice.

Chapter Twenty-Four

"I'M GLAD YOU told me." Tuesday morning Trinity adjusts the row of ceramic teapots that line half a wall to point all the spouts toward the door. "These need to be angled like this, for good luck."

"I think that applies to elephants. I'm not so sure about teapots." I have to admit, though, that the eclectic collection pops after her quick revamp. "Since when are you about fortune? Isn't your job all about the facts?" I've spent the last half hour telling her all that I've figured out. Which isn't a whole lot, if looking at *just the facts*.

"It is, but one can never underestimate the human instinct."

"To kill?" I hand her a teapot that I wasn't sure where to put as it's square, from the UK, and looks nothing like the others. "It'll fit in fine now, with the spout angled with the others."

Trinity smiles. "Maybe I should quit the force and be your shop assistant."

"You'd last an hour, tops. The first time a customer complained you'd tell them to pound sand."

"Pretty much, yeah. And no, not the instinct to harm one another. That's not natural, unless it's a protection thing. The scariest people I've ever faced have been a mother or father thinking they had to protect their child from me or one of my colleagues."

"I totally get that." I know I'd lay down my life to protect Ava and Lilly. And take the bad guy with me.

"I'm talking about gut instinct. I'm under the impression the Navy taught you to ignore it a lot of the time."

"Not ignore it but keep it in its place. During pilot training and follow-on certifications, instinct always made me want to panic when I was blindfolded, underwater, strapped into an upside-down helo frame. Solid training allowed me to stay calm, focused. Wait for the helo to settle at the bottom of the pool. Then I was able to unbuckle and let buoyancy get me out and up to the water's surface."

"Well, in police work it's a little different. No, make that a lot. We face life or death every day, depending upon our beat and assignments. A good cop always listens to their instincts. But don't take it the wrong way; everything has to be backed up by facts."

"It sounds like you're not any closer to solving Frannie's murder than—" I stop myself before my arrogance shoves my foot into my mouth.

Trinity's brow raises simultaneously with the side of her mouth. "Go on. You were saying?"

"I'm sorry. I know I'm not the expert here, believe me."

"You just can't help yourself, Angel. You wouldn't have the successful career behind you, or the one to look forward to here, if you weren't driven."

"Are you okay with me talking to Liza?" I purposefully don't ask if she or anyone at SPD has contacted the former assistant. Because, when it comes down to it, I don't want to do anything to jeopardize it getting solved. I can handle an ego blow for not figuring it out myself.

"I don't see that it's a problem. One of my detectives made contact with her, and her supervisors. Her alibi is the most solid of everyone's so far."

"The living in Namibia part?" I manage to draw a snort out of Trinity.

"Yes. Just make sure you don't disclose anything about the investigation that you're aware of. The last think we need is Cornelia Applebaum telling her friends that we have a suspect, when we don't."

"How could I tell her that when, um, *we* don't?"

"Trust me, the most basic facts in a murder investigation can turn into gossip fodder with zero effort from you." Trinity speaks with conviction.

"Okay, got it. I can talk to Liza, but keep it to what her experience was while working for Frannie and Ken."

"Leave out the having an affair with Ken part, maybe. See what she brings up on her own."

"Are you giving me expert tips on interrogation, Detective Colson?"

"Don't push it."

NATE'S COMING TO pick me up for our date at seven tonight, and it's already after five. Even though it's past midnight in Namibia, Liza insisted we do our FaceTime now because "my WiFi is too unpredictable at any other time."

I've set up my personal tablet in the shop office, and Ralph's content on his portable perch, chewing on a stick. The building settles around me as the sun's been down for over an hour, and a strong wind is coming in from the north. A nor'easter is brewing and we're predicted to have snow by Thanksgiving. Enough to make everything look like Christmas has arrived early, but not enough to keep customers away on Saturday.

My stomach pitches and rolls as I stare at my tablet, willing Liza to call. It's all I can do to not make the call myself, but best to let her run the show on our connection. A tip from Trinity. It will make Liza more comfortable to speak to me, instead of coming across as invading her space.

"*Eeeetch.*" Ralph doesn't scream his mystery word, but his gaze is intent on something in the shop. He can see straight through to the front window and I'm sure he's complaining about the passersby. Stonebridge has come alive these past evenings since the town's Christmas lights are up, with matching green glitter garland tree silhouettes on every lamppost. All the small businesses, mine included, have an oversized red bow atop their display window, with the ribbon ends hanging to flap in the wind.

Excitement about the opening swirls with my nerves over knowing the killer is still out there, and maybe a bit of anticipation for tonight's dinner with Nate. Before I can go into that dark neighborhood in my mind where the killer finds me before I find them and Nate stands me up, the tablet lights up with Liza's call.

I suck in a deep breath, paste a smile on, and press Accept.

It takes longer than it does with Ava or Lily, but within seconds Liza's face appears. She's remarkably pretty, with long brunette hair and bright eyes.

"Liza, hi!"

"Hey." Her smile is warm, but her eyes narrow a bit. I don't blame her.

"I can't thank you enough for agreeing to talk to me. Your grandmother tells me your schedule is crazy over there!"

"Oh, if you know my grandma, she's never going to say anything other than how great one of her grandkids are." She laughs, and it comes across as sincere, full-bodied.

"You're probably wondering why I asked to speak with you."

"Not at all. It's about Frannie Schrock, right? I stay up-to-date from my family, of course, and I go on PennLive to get all the deets on Stonebridge." She mentions the central Pennsylvania news site.

"Yes. I'm sure you know, then, that she was killed in my building."

"Yeah, Grandma told me. Right in your shop, and you haven't even opened yet. That's awful."

"It's not great, but nothing compared to what happened to Frannie."

"I was horrified when I heard. I used to work for both of them, Ken and Frannie, as you know. They are, *were*, complicated to say the least. Either one of them have reasons for people to be angry at them. But to actually murder Frannie? I have to think it was random. Is there any possibility of that?"

"Sure, from what the police tell me, there's always that chance." But Frannie's murder was very personal, by all indications. Indicators that Liza doesn't seem to know about. A good thing for the security of the investigation.

"You don't think so, do you?" Liza's intelligent observation gives me pause.

"I, I don't know, Liza. I'm a retired Navy pilot, an empty nester. My girls aren't much younger than you—they just went off to college. I'm not here in an official capacity at all." I cross my fingers. I'm not lying but being buds with SPD's lead detective makes me as official as any unofficial person can be by now.

"So you're interested in my time with Ken and Frannie,

working at the shop?" She flips her hair over a shoulder. "Well, it was fine, until I got personally involved. If you don't know already, you will soon enough. I had an affair with Ken. According to him, I'm the only one he ever stepped out on Frannie with. And you know what? I believed him when he told me that. Frannie had the ability to get a little unhinged over their business dealings. Ken is more easygoing."

"Who broke it off?"

"There was nothing to break off. It was very brief, I was young and naïve, and if I hadn't been stupid with Ken, it would have been with someone else. I was on the rebound from a long-term breakup."

"How did Frannie find out?"

"I've never known how. But as soon as she did, she and Ken had a huge fight. Nothing physical, or trust me, one of us would have called the cops."

"Who else heard their fight, besides you?"

"There was only ever the two of us, me and Jenna, in the office most of the time. The other realtors came and went, busy with listing and showing properties."

"And after the fight Frannie fired you?"

"Oh, no. It was my decision. I think they were both afraid of a lawsuit. With me being an employee and all, it was a sticky situation. Maybe I'll think differently when I get older, but I wasn't manipulated by Ken in any way. He was at a low point in his marriage, and I was young and dumb." I stare at her still very young face and admire the wisdom she's acquired.

"Did you know Jenna's still there?"

"I'm sure she is." Liza shakes her head. "I was there for just under a year, and I left two years ago. Jenna was supposed to be a temporary hire. She came on about a month after me. I'm sorry to hear she's still there, but I'm not surprised."

"Why is that? How Frannie treated her?"

"No, not at all. Jenna was willing to put up with whatever it took to stay there."

"Really?"

"It used to drive me nuts, seeing her deal with Frannie's temper. We all suffered from it, but I always knew I wasn't going to stay there forever, a year at most. It was a waypoint as I figured out what I wanted to do next with my life. My relationship with Ken was an awkward thing but not like it is for Jenna."

"What do you mean?"

"Oh my goodness. Now, this a bit of gossip, and things may have changed, but Jenna isn't how she seems. She's totally professional, never does anything at all that could be considered out of line. She's loyal to a fault."

"But?"

"But she had the most humongous crush on Ken. To be fair, I could have stayed on after Frannie found out. It would have been awkward, and it wouldn't say much about me as a person if I'd stayed, but I didn't feel forced out by either Frannie or Ken. Jenna made it so uncomfortable. She was truly shattered when she found out. I could tell by how she sniffled around the office, wouldn't make eye contact with me. No, leaving was the best thing for all concerned. No question." She leans back, and I see her twin bed in the background. "Anything else?"

"Gosh, no. You've been so generous with your time. I can't thank you enough for sharing this with me, Liza." Although it's not gleaned a whole lot. So Jenna had a crush on her boss. Not uncommon, especially in the Schrock Real Estate office.

After brief niceties, we disconnect.

I might have stumbled upon a motive for murder. Jenna's crush on Ken. But I still don't have the murderer. Jenna's alibi was investigated by both SPD and me, albeit SPD was far more thorough than me. I only spoke to Allie at Suds & Sparkles, whereas I'm certain Trinity covered all of the shops where Jenna claimed to have been that afternoon.

I have less than an hour to close up shop and grab a quick shower before I expect Nate.

"Come on, buddy boy." Ralph adroitly hops onto my shoulder and we head upstairs.

Chapter Twenty-Five

I STAY UNDER the hot shower a little longer than I intended, but the spray offers me comfort and it's exactly the
space I need to review everything I know about Frannie's
murder to date. My date outfit is laid out on my bed, and
I've put my hair in a shower cap so that I won't have to do
anything with it. I washed it last night and with it so long it's
easy to do a quick updo.

Hot water pulses between my shoulders as I hug myself
and let my head hang, getting the crick out of my neck. I
may not have solved Frannie's murder, yet, but I have the
satisfaction of knowing I've actually helped Trinity and SPD
without messing anything up. Trinity's the best at her job,
and I'll be more thrilled than she when she gets answers. I
just wish it would be sooner than later.

The conversation with Liza keeps buzzing around my
brain. She was correct; I'd never have figured out that Jenna
has a crush on Ken. Except…Jenna was very attentive to him
in those first days after the murder. Protective. More than
your average executive assistant, I'd say. Of course, office
relationships can become familial, I'd guess. Not unlike the

Navy.

The biggest contributions I've made to the case for Trinity have to be that Max confided in me about his affair with Frannie, that they broke up on Saturday. And by speaking to Liza, I figured out that Jenna had the hots for Ken, long-term. That has to help, right? I need to tell Trinity all of this. There's time to call and at least leave her voicemail before Nate shows up.

The thought of my date makes the butterfly residents in my stomach trill their wings in giddy anticipation.

"Calm down, girlfriend." I talk to myself when I'm nervous.

I turn off the water and open the door to get my towel.

"*Eeeetch! UUUUU eeeeetch!*"

"Quiet, Ralph!" It's as if he knows I have an important event tonight. I'm trying to believe it's nothing more than a low-key dinner, but it's with a man who isn't Tom. And the first one I've been so drawn to. Amazing how much can happen in a little more than a week. The Saturday morning before Frannie died, I didn't even know Nate existed. And the biggest surprise to me was when Max showed up at...

At back shop door. Surprised to see me. As if...

"*We broke up on Saturday.*" Max's words, when he wouldn't meet my eyes.

Had Max planned to meet Frannie *here* last Saturday? I thought briefly he could have been the killer, but after my conversations with him and Trinity's investigation, he'd already have revealed himself to be the killer. But he was dressed for a lot more than construction when he showed up at my back door. And hadn't he intimated that the breakup happened sooner than he'd thought it would? Had he and Frannie had one last…fling…before she broke it off?

I shake away the image of them doing anything of the sort in the back storeroom. The cold memory of Frannie's body is enough. But I can't stop my thoughts from tumbling together, determined to coalesce into logic.

"I don't know how Frannie found out about Ken and I." Liza's words.

"Meet me. I'll text you where." Frannie to Jenna, in front of Latte Love, the last time I saw Frannie alive.

"Uuuuu eeeetch!" Ralph's screech interrupts my problem-solving mode. He's on a tear, as if he can sense my agitation. What should be elation, really.

Because I think I've solved it.

"Eeeetch! Eeeetch!"

"Ralph! Give me a minute."

"Uuuuu weeeetch." He won't quit. But this last yell of his, it's lower, more…human. When he wants to, Ralph can eerily mimic a specific person's voice.

It's not *b-eeeetch*, but *weeeeeetch*. Ralph's really good at consonants and would delight in saying *bitch* if he ever heard it. No, it's not *b-eeetch*.

It's witch. *You witch!* In a voice I recognize, should have recognized days ago. A soft, definitely female voice.

There's one common denominator, one person, in all of this. I wrap the large towel around me and grab my phone, on the bathroom counter. Trinity's on speed dial, which my shaking fingers appreciate.

"Come on, come on." Several rings, then it goes to voicemail. I groan, then leave my message. "Hey, it's me. Look, I know you're going to think I'm crazy, but the one person who deserves another look is—"

"Put the phone down, Angel." I jump, clutch the towel to my chest. I stare at the gun pointed to my chest, look up into the eyes of a very manipulative woman.

The killer.

"Jenna." I say her name, loudly, before I drop the phone on the counter, praying she doesn't see I didn't disconnect. With luck, I can get her to confess and it'll be on Trinity's voicemail. I hold my hands up. My towel drops. Great. I have to negotiate with a murderer, and stay alive, while naked.

You've done Navy SERE training. Survival, Evasion, Resistance, Escape.

"Please, Jenna. Let's talk. We can work this out."

"*Uuuuu Eeeetch*!" Ralph doesn't think so.

"Shut up and get your stupid bird to do the same. Now." Jenna looks nothing like the subdued assistant tonight. For one, she's dressed in all black. Great. Probably stalked me while I, oblivious, floated up here in anticipation of going out with Nate.

Poor Nate. I doubt he's ever found a naked, dead date instead of one all dressed up to meet him. Or undressed, of co—

"Don't you hear me?" Jenna waves the gun and the glint in her eyes reminds me of the glass shards left in Frannie's. The reminder of Frannie's undeserved, horrible death opens the door to sheer outrage. My legs and arms begin to shake and I clench my fists.

Get her talking.

"I hear you, Jenna. I know you're going to kill me, so at least tell me something before you do. You killed Frannie, didn't you?"

"I hadn't planned on it. It was a mistake! I got mad, is all."

"Why were you so angry?"

"She treated Ken like dirt!"

"That wasn't new, though. What did she do this time?"

"I saw her. With him."

"With whom?"

"That low-life handyman you hired!"

"Max." It all clicks into place. She'd walked in on them when they were together. Max had admitted their rendezvous to me.

"Yeah, yeah, Max!" She screams his name in the scariest pitch I've ever heard. She's shaking all over and I know I'm closer to death than I've ever been. I have to stay cool, calm. For the girls. For my family. For me.

"Listen to me, Jenna. You just described a crime of passion. No jury will ever convict you for that." My new lying habit that's come easily with a barrel in my face.

"No, they won't, because I'm not going to get caught. You had no idea I know you've been snooping all over town about this, did you?"

I'd only just figured out she was the killer, so why would I think she was paying attention to me? Not the time for a wisecrack reply, though. "That's just it, Jenna you will get caught. Detective Colson is already on the way over." Another lie. "So what, you're going to take me out now, too? To what end?"

Her head rears back, the handgun lowers a few inches. Jenna's not immune to my words. *Good.*

"Frannie wasn't good for this town. You don't see that but everyone else does. She was evil, a real witch! Things will be much nicer here with her gone." She takes a breath, re-aims. "Now, move, before I finish you in here."

Slowly I back out of the bathroom, never moving my gaze from her weapon. My Navy training has finally kicked in. I know this because it's like I'm watching myself go through the motions, while calculating whether it'd be best to kick the gun out of her hands, or duck and tackle her. I'm not going to allow her to fire at me point blank.

And she's not going to, or she already would have. Jenna might still change her mind.

"Why don't you put the gun down, Jenna, and let's talk

this out. I know it's been so hard on you. All of this."

"Damn right it has."

My legs hit the table at the back of my sofa, which faces the fireplace. When I bump into it, the keys rattle in their bowl. Jenna's between me and the front door, my only viable escape. She left the front door open, no doubt so I wouldn't hear the door shut. Ralph's shivering inside his cage, between the living room and kitchen.

"How did you break in, Jenna?" I'd changed all the locks.

"You didn't throw your bolt, you stupid jerk."

"Silly me." I make it a point to look over my shoulder. "I can't go any further here, Jenna."

"*Uuuuuuu weeeeetch*!" Ralph lets out his loudest yell ever, which makes Jenna jump.

And gives me a chance to live.

Before Jenna takes her attention from Ralph I dive for her legs, knocking her flat. The gun goes off, followed by plaster falling from the ceiling. I hit her with such force that I roll past her, to the front door. I scramble to my feet but she's already on hers, and she's waving the gun around like it's a sparkler.

I grab the Santa figurine from his spot next to the front door and throw it at her face. "Take that, you witch!"

"Hey!" A shot fires, Jenna screams. "I'm going to kill you!"

I'm already running out the door, angled for the stairwell. I'll jump down the entire flight if I have to.

"Oof." I hit a hard wall before I reach the first stair. Arms go around me, hold me close. I try to escape. I have to keep running!

"It's okay. You're safe. We got her." Words murmured into my ear. The familiar deep timbre cuts through my adrenaline rush.

I look up. "Nate?"

He carefully turns me around so that I can see my front door. Open wide, with Trinity in the threshold. She's posed with her legs wide, pistol hot and between her steady hands.

As soon as Trinity lowers and holsters her weapon, Nate and I take a step closer. As Trinity calls for EMTs, we learn why. Jenna is sitting on the floor in front of Ralph's cage, my beloved Russian Santa with a bullet hole through his center on its back next to her. Jenna's moaning, holding her right shoulder. She'll live to stand trial.

A rustling behind me makes me jump. But it's just Nate, shrugging out of his parka and wrapping it around me.

I'd forgotten I was naked.

"Nate, I was in the shower—"

"It's okay, Angel." The glimmer of appreciation in his eyes tells me that it is, indeed, okay. All of it. So Nate saw my hiney—no biggie. Well, I mean, my butt's not the smallest—

Pounding footsteps heralds a uniformed officer, who walks up behind Trinity. At her nod and hand motion,

Officer Sam McCloud retrieves Jenna's weapon from next to my sofa. With zero sign of nausea.

Before I allow myself to look at Ralph's cage more closely, I say a quick prayer. What are the chances a bullet ricocheted into his birdie heart?

Slim to nil, apparently, as he's sitting on his heated perch, moving from one claw to the other. His version of pacing. His sweet green head is bobbing up and down, as if he's trying to find the words to express all that's unfolded in front of him. Again. Until he sees me in the doorway.

"Mommy's home!"

"I NEVER WOULD have been caught if not for her." Jenna practically spits the words, refusing to look my way. She's sitting up on a gurney, being tended to by EMTs, who have already bandaged her shoulder and put her on oxygen. Her hands are handcuffed in front of her, as are her ankles.

Trinity arrested her for the murder of Frannie Schrock, for breaking and entering, plus attempted murder of me. I'm standing back from it all, still wrapped in Nate's parka. Nate hasn't left my side, nor taken his arm from around my shoulders.

"You may want to wait for your lawyer, Jenna." Trinity's stern warning tells me all I need to know. SPD has enough evidence to allow the DA to prosecute Jenna, and for the

Judge to put her away for a long while.

"It doesn't matter. I did it out of anger. It was a crime of passion. I know the law." Jenna turns her head, her gaze searching until she finds me. Pure contempt glows from her eyes. "You ruined it all. You want Ken to yourself."

I shake my head while Nate grips my shoulder more firmly. I look up at him. "There's nothing—"

"I know."

"You do?"

"Yes." He nods. Warmth curls in my belly, dispels the last of the fright shudders that have racked my frame since Jenna pointed her weapon at me.

"That's enough, Jenna." Trinity looks at the EMTs. "Officer McCloud will be with her 24/7."

"Yes, ma'am." They nod, slowly wheel Jenna out of the room. Is it possible that this ugly anomaly of my hometown life is finally over?

Chapter Twenty-Six

"**Y**OUR QUICK THINKING saved your life, and helped us take Jenna into custody sooner than we might have." Trinity's drinking from my DON'T MESS WITH A FEMALE VETERAN mug, and the sentiment is apropos to her, too. Don't mess with the most badass detective in Pennsylvania. After Jenna was cuffed and read her rights, she was taken away on a stretcher with a 24/7 police escort. I am no longer naked under Nate's parka but in my softest, coziest rose pink flannel pajamas. The ones with green parrots printed on them. While I was dressing, I called Crystal and caught her up on what happened. Which is why she's ensconced at the end of the table, mug in hand.

A forensics team is still at work in my living room, but for now I have all I need gathered around my kitchen table. Trinity, Mom and Dad, and Ralph, who's refused to leave my shoulder. Nate sits on the kitchen stepladder stool, observing our interaction. He made us all a big pot of coffee. No one's going to sleep any time soon.

"Had you already figured out it was Jenna?" I pose the question to Trinity, and watch all heads turn toward her.

"I was close, but not one hundred percent convinced until I heard your voicemail."

A grin, the first of the night, tugs at my mouth. "You mean I cracked the case?"

Mom gasps and Dad rolls his eyes, pats Mom's hand. "Please don't encourage her, Trinity." But Dad's tone is full of pride. Love.

Trinity bites her lower lip but can't hold back her laughter. She nods. "Yes."

"While I appreciate that, dear friend," I hold my mug up in a toast, "I am not interested in being involved in a crime of any kind ever again." And most especially, not a murder. No thank you.

"If it's at all up to me, and the entire SPD team, you won't be." Trinity's comment triggers a round of laughter, a release from the night's terror.

"I mean it. I left the Navy to pursue a different kind of passion. A way to bring the world to small-town America." Funny thing, though. When I say *passion* I sneak a quick look at Nate. He catches my gaze and…smiles.

"To be fair, you provided enough information to keep the case going when we were stymied. Jenna was very thorough and left zero prints behind. Not one strand of hair." Trinity's pulls her battered notebook from her pocked and flips through the pages one at a time. "There are several strong suspects. And I had no idea that even the possibility of an ancient ruin existing here could be the source of criminal behavior."

"But the eel weir ended up having nothing to do with Frannie's murder." I'm interested in seeing if the V-shaped rock formation in Jacob's Run is indeed ancient. And I like that it won't be associated with Frannie's murder.

"No, but it gives SPD reason to keep our eyes and ears open. Stonebridge could literally be sitting on—"

"A historic discovery never before seen in central Pennsylvania!" Mom's enthusiasm is reborn. Dad and I exchange looks. We are going to hear all about the weir again, whether we want to or not.

Trinity doesn't bother to continue her thoughts on the weir. But what I hear is that Stonebridge isn't the sleepy town I grew up in. There are outside events and forces that we have no control over.

But for tonight, with my family and friends surrounding me, Frannie's murder solved and the killer apprehended, Stonebridge is the safest place I've ever known besides Tom's arms. I can still feel his embrace as never before, but with a difference. Tom would be happy for me, and Nate is the exact kind of man he'd want me to fall for.

Because yes, I think I've fallen for the man who's persisted in trying to spend time with me, all the while I've been dealing with a hot mess.

I'm going to keep my personal revelation to myself for now. It's enough to know the murder has been solved.

WEDNESDAY MORNING AFTER Jenna's arrest is the brightest I've woken to since moving home and it's still pre-dawn. I've never been this alert on only a few hours of sleep. The forensics team wrapped up by two A.M., after which Trinity okayed me to stay in my home.

I'm emotionally exhausted, for sure, but I know it'll pass. My home is safe and my chicks are flying back to the nest. Or, rather, Mom and Dad are going to get Ava and Lily today. We all decided it's still best for them to get the girls, so that I can catch my breath and get the last of the shop's preparations finished before our family Thanksgiving dinner.

Nate spent the night, along with Mach. No, not like that. Nate was on the sofa (he refused to mess up either of the girl's rooms) and Mach alternated between the living room and my bedroom, next to Ralph's cage. I caved and let Ralph bunk in my room, just for the night.

Nate said there was no way he'd leave me alone after such a scare. We're definitely in the earliest parts of whatever our relationship is going to be. But I will forever be grateful to him for being so supportive and kind last night, and these first weeks of our acquaintance.

I brush my teeth and head into the front of the apartment. The sofa is empty, and there's no sign of Mach. Did Nate leave?

"Good morning." He calls from the kitchen, across the

living room. It's a relief to hear his voice. In the best way.

I walk to the kitchen and slide into a chair. "Morning."

Nate's heating milk for cappuccinos on my stove, using the old-fashioned frother I bought in Italy. A traditional espresso pot gurgles on the smallest burner. Mach's under the table, but he stirs enough to curl at my feet, firmly resting his snout on my slippered feet.

"Where's Ralph? I thought he'd be on your shoulder."

"Are you kidding? He's a sloth in the fall and winter. Don't try to get him to come out from under his cage cover before the sun's up."

Nate laughs, pours the espresso, and then pumps the frothing pot until the milk has doubled. He takes the seat across from mine. Our gazes meet and I wonder if my eyes are crinkling like his.

"Some first date, huh?" I sip the coffee. "Nate, this is so good."

"It was the best first date. Not the killer breaking into your home bit. But being able to share a life experience with you." He points to his coffee. "I used the coffee in your cupboard and the milk from your refrigerator."

"I know, but there's something so nice about someone else making it for me." Except I know it has nothing to do with someone else and everything to do with Nate.

I could get used to this. And one other thing—not having to look over my shoulder for a killer.

Chapter Twenty-Seven

Small Business Saturday
Grand Opening

"I'M SO IN love with your store!" The young mother with a baby strapped to her chest smiles as I wrap the Japanese watercolor prints in red-and-green tissue paper before placing them in a paper gift bag with SHOP 'ROUND THE WORLD imprinted over an etched drawing of the shop. It's two hours into the grand opening and the cash register tells me that we've already rung up fifty-three sales. If the touchpad made sounds like the antique English cash register I have for sale in the far corner, where I've begun a display of international collectibles that I've found locally, the ringing would be nonstop.

"I'm so glad! Please stop in again." I hand her the bag, the handles tied together with a festive plaid bow. "Next!"

I've been standing here for the last twenty minutes as my main cashiers for today—Ava and Lily—needed a break and are in my office, where I've set out a smaller version of the food I'm offering out here. Crystal, Bryce, and Nico will stop by later, after closing their shops. We're going to have a family party here in the retail space.

"I'll take this one, and do you have any other sport Santas in the back?" Red plunks down one of the figures, and I can't help but remember how a similar wooden carving stuck out of Frannie's chest.

Nope. Not going there.

"I'll have to check. Are there any other teams you're interested in?"

"The Eagles, of course." He nods, then stills. "You know, Angel, I sure am sorry if you got the impression anyone on the Stonebridge Buddies thought you were to blame for Frannie's death. I'm so glad you're safe and sound, and that Trinity caught the killer." He shakes his head. "Jenna, the mouse of Main Street, who would have thought? Guess there's no telling what lust can do."

"You're right, Red." I call over to my Dad and have him check in the back for more sports Santas while I wrap the order.

"Here you go, Red." Dad hands Red a Russian Santa painted in green and white.

"Fantastic! My kids will be happy." He leans over the register. "Do you have anything my wife would like? She's a nut about Christmas."

I lead Red over to the German Christmas display and suggest either a carved nativity or a candle mobile. While he ponders his decision, I head back to the counter. After I ring up two more customers that include yet more local business owners, there's a lull in the line as shoppers *ooh* and *aah* over the merchandise. Mom and Dad appear to be having the time of their lives. In fact, we're all over-the-top happy, and why wouldn't we be? The store is finally open, a crime has been solved and the criminal will face justice in county court.

Nate looks up from where he's busy making mini-lattes for the crowd. He's dispensed them into three-ounce cups, and sprinkles gold and silver sugar on the foam. He grins and I respond in kind.

"Mom, the apple strudel is to die for." Ava speaks with food in her mouth, powdered sugar raining onto her green holiday sweater.

"Close your mouth, sis." Lilly walks up next to her, hands her twin a paper napkin with tiny red poinsettias printed on it. "You look like a piggy."

And that's the cue. They explode into their trademark giggles, turning heads and stirring up random laughs from the crowd.

"How's Ralph doing back there?"

Ava sobers. "He's fine, Mom. It was a good call to keep him in your office."

"Yeah, it's way too busy out here." Lily agrees.

I nod. "I'll have him out here with me on regular business days. But not today!"

The sleigh bells on the door jingle and Trinity walks in, her family in tow. I rush around the counter and hug her before she can catch her breath.

"Thank you so much for stopping in!"

"You're kidding, right? I'd never miss your big day."

"I know you wouldn't." We smile at each other, and it's right then that I know. Trinity and I are going to be good friends again. The best.

Nate must have judged the crowd and walks over to us, hands me my personal mug.

"Exactly what I need about now." It's only been a few hours since I had my last sip of coffee, but the last days have caught up with me. I don't speak as I lift the mug to my lips. And halt, mug midair, after I glance at the latte art.

The outline of a large dog with a large bird on its head is surrounded by the sugar sprinkles. A laugh starts in the vicinity of my heart and rolls up, up and out of my mouth. Followed by another. And another. Until I'm laughing so hard I'm out of control.

The girls stare. Mom and Dad stop what they're doing. They're all probably thinking that it's all finally gotten to me. This is my meltdown after so much angst.

Tears blur the store's twinkle lights. Ever since Frannie's murder was solved, Jenna arrested, and the girls have come home, I've been an emotional wreck. And certainly all that's transpired would make anyone feel shaky, out of sorts. Not to mention launching a new business. But my sense of vulnerability isn't from Shop 'Round the World, either.

My vulnerability isn't scary or heavy. It's joy-centered.

Stonebridge has embraced me, and my fellow citizens

and business owners no longer think I'm a criminal. I have a guy who might become a steady part of my life. I have my family. I've mended fences with my high school BFF, and we're picking up where we left off. It's so good to have a best friend once more. Even though she may or may not have warned me off ever getting involved in her investigations again.

But how likely is another murder in Stonebridge, Pennsylvania?

The End

Want more? Don't miss Angel's next adventure in
A Mid-Summer Murder!

Join Tule Publishing's newsletter for more great reads and weekly deals!

Acknowledgements

It's a bold step to change genres, and as the author of over thirty romance novels, it was scary and exhilarating to step into the genre of my heart. I owe this writing breakthrough to my agent Emily Sylvan Kim, without whose fierce loyalty and dogged determination my work would be unpolished and unsold. Thank you, Emily, from the bottom of my heart. Many thanks and fist bumps to publisher Jane Porter and her entire Tule team for taking a chance on me and inspiring me to write my best book. I'm forever grateful. Many thanks to my editor Sinclair Sawhney who doesn't hesitate to ask me to dig deeper. Most importantly, thank you dear reader for your unwavering support and enthusiasm as you discovered I was entering the mystery world. I do it for you.

If you enjoyed *A Santa Stabbing,*
you'll love the next book in the...

Shop 'Round the World series

Book 1: *A Santa Stabbing*

Book 2: *A Mid-Summer Murder*
Coming in April 2023

Available now at your favorite online retailer!

Book Club Questions

1. What did you like best about *A Santa Stabbing*?

2. What bothered you the most about *A Santa Stabbing*?

3. Did you like Angel as a sleuth?

4. Do you relate to Angel changing careers mid-life?

5. If you were going to make a television series from this book and the series, who would you cast as Angel? As Trinity? As Nate?

6. Have you read other Geri Krotow books? How is this book different?

7. Would you read another book by Geri Krotow?

8. What is your favorite thing about Stonebridge?

9. Did you like the animal characters? Did you like Ralph the bird or Mach the Shiloh better, and why?

10. Are you looking forward to the next Shop 'Round the World book? What would you like to see more or less of throughout this series?

About the Author

Geri Krotow is the bestselling author of over 25 novels of romantic suspense, contemporary romance and women's fiction. A US Naval Academy graduate and Navy veteran, Geri's strong heroines are reader favorites. Geri's Shop 'Round the World series with Tule is her cozy mystery debut.

Thank you for reading

A Santa Stabbing

If you enjoyed this book, you can find more from all our great authors at TulePublishing.com, or from your favorite online retailer.

TULE
PUBLISHING

9 781958 686386